THE DEWEY DECIMAL SYSTEM

A NOVEL BY

NATHAN LARSON

This is a work of fiction. All names, characters, places, and incidents are the product of the author's imagination. Any resemblance to real events or persons, living or dead, is entirely coincidental.

Published by Akashic Books

ISBN-13: 978-1-61775-010-6
Library of Congress Control Number: 2010939101

First printing

Akashic Books
PO Box 1456
New York, NY 10009
info@akashicbooks.com
www.akashicbooks.com

THE DEWEY DECIMAL SYSTEM

To my wife and son

And I wake, gasping and flailing at the hooded shapes that recede swiftly with my sleep, the report of the gunshot ricocheting off my skull and out into the great hall of the Reading Room.

Always the same dream.

As the sound fades and the hush returns by degrees to that massive chamber, my heart rate slows and indeed I know exactly where I am: the Main Branch of the New York Public Library at the juncture of 42nd Street and Fifth Avenue, in the City of New York.

I can't relate in exact detail what led me here, but this much I can tell you: I am a man of mixed ethnicity, from the borough of the Bronx. I freelance from time to time for the government of the City of New York. Or at least what's left of it.

I am, or was, a soldier, in a landscape without features, save for the funnels of sand the wind might kick up, and the occasional cluster of low buildings. In this antispace there were long periods of time where nothing whatsoever occurred, and we were very hot. When shit did happen, it did so very fast, in a flourish of blood and bits of metal and fiberglass. Even so, it all seemed so very half-assed. Hard to take seriously.

Like a bad movie you didn't really want to watch, but settled on for lack of options.

And, you know, I was a husband and a father. I think. But that was before.

I sit up, rifle through my suit jacket for a cigarette, and find none. Despite the relative quiet, I'm not alone here . . . a mother and son have an old hot plate going nearby, staring intently into the pot, mother holding a potato aloft, presumably waiting for the water to boil.

I'm surprised they found a working outlet. Take stock of its location should I need to charge my shaver. This might be one of the last public buildings that draws off of the city's skeletal power grid.

Have a job here at the library. I'm taking care of the books. But more about that later.

Beyond the Madonna and child, other human forms are scattered here and there, adrift and irrelevant.

Irrelevant, that sounds cold. But for as much as the city has been transformed, there's one thing that's truer than it ever was in this town, and that's this: if you don't have a direct line, a Batphone, you not going to make it.

I, people, have a direct line.

Speaking of which, my pager hums. It's the DA. Check the code: tells me I need to get down to the office pronto.

Hop up, fasten my belt. Spritz on a little Purell™ and wring my hands. Purell™ is a must-have go-to kind of thing for me, a cool breeze in a hot world of crazy.

I sleep in my suit: fuck it. Saves time. Step into my wing tips, roll up my bedding, shove it all into my army-issue bag, and stow it on a low shelf with my jerky, stash of pistachios, and bottled water.

Nobody will so much as touch my gear. They know who I am, and, more importantly, they know who I know.

Dry swallowing my wake-up pill, I'm down the worn

marble stairs and out into the piss-warm drizzle; I slap on my hat and tap the northernmost lion's stone haunch as I pass by.

This is part of my System. Left on Fifth Avenue. All important, to follow the System. And use Purell™, especially after you've touched a public edifice.

Rain mutes the pervading odor of burning plastic and garbage. Midsummer, indeed the first summer after the events of February 14.

The smell loiters even now, reliable as death; that's the plastic. The trash odor stems from the waste holes in what was once Bryant Park.

In accordance with the System I take the left on 42nd Street. Prior to 11 a.m. I will only execute left turns. Headed to the B train.

Show my laminate to the female Marine, she bids me proceed, and I descend.

Improbably, the subway soldiers on, thanks to federal funds earmarked for the "Great Reconstruction." Exactly who is responsible for allocating the cash within the city is unknown to me, but I can tell you it ain't done with the public good in mind. First priority would be lining the pockets of many a shady character downtown, as well as the various construction warlords who swarmed the island post–2/14.

That's the real, and no effort is made whatsoever to disguise this fact.

Subway service (now fully automated) is strictly reserved for city employees, dignitaries, and those who are liquid enough to lay a healthy donation across the right sweaty palm. Trust me, such folks are few and far between. Plus, if you can hang with such heavy bribery, why the fuck would you be taking the freaking subway? Chances are you've already headed inland and are holed up behind gates at a compound upstate, or in central Jersey. Away from the water, away from possible future "occurrences." God bless.

Some of us need to work. Some of us have a System.

Just me on the platform. The water looks to be about ankle deep on the tracks, rats paddle by in schools. The very sight of them makes me reach for that Purell™ again.

A D train, then an F, piloted by some distant computer. I board the B when it pulls in.

The System protects me, keeps my thoughts structured. There are rules, sure: When riding the New York City subway, it's essential to begin with letter trains (A, B, C), and then only in alphabetic order. If traveling more than four stops, it's essential to transfer to a number train (1, 2, 3), and in a perfect world the first transfer should be an even number.

It's no disaster if that's not a possibility, I'm just saying: the more you work the System, the more the System works for you. For this reason I switch to the 6 train at Broadway/Lafayette.

I share a car with a group of Transit Authority cops. Uniforms mismatched. The biggest one gives me the once-over, clocks the laminate, nods in my direction.

I touch the brim of my hat. It's an effort to keep my face composed. Funny, no? After everything I've been subjected to, to the limited extent I can remember particulars, I'm jumpy around cops.

I take my pulse and count backward from ten, employing the System. Exiting at Canal, I exhale, feeling the cops' eyes on the back of my neck.

I'm thinking I need to double up, so I pop another pill and emerge into the hot haze, the dank barnyard of Chinatown.

No exaggeration: I'm kicking aside chickens as I move south on Lafayette, handkerchief to my lips. Solid petri-dish stuff, a misting of bird flu, swine flu, dog flu, mad cow, tuberculosis, and worse. Look-alike faces swarm and jabber. SARS masks.

I might be fluent in Cantonese but that doesn't mean I want to stop and have a conversation.

I finger the single key in my front pocket.

And, needless to say, I whip out the Purell™.

Using a System-based technique I block out the human static and meditate on today's possible activities.

Our current and unelected district attorney is Daniel Rosenblatt, a mouth-breathing, weak-jawed, beta male–type individual who seems to demand righteous abuse.

In the military we called such types (though they were rare) "canaries" (see "canary in a coal mine," see also "cannon fodder"). Best uses of such a person include minesweeping, drawing sniper fire away from more useful personnel, and disposal of unexploded ordinance.

Not that I care but I think Rosenblatt was a once a staff lawyer at one of those 1-800-VICTIM2 outfits. Ambulance-chasing type stuff. In the post-Valentine's chaos, there was a lot of general upheaval, shuffling, many power grabs. And Rosenblatt somehow planted his ass here.

Despite appearances, we all know it's exactly this type of man who can be the most dangerous, given a corner office. An office like this one, here on the nineteenth floor at 100 Centre Street. Art deco appointments. Southwest facing; out the sooty windows one has a decent view of the recently reinstated Freedom Tower construction site. The blighted remains of the Brooklyn Bridge are just visible behind City Hall, awaiting the healing balm of the Great Reconstruction.

It's quite a view.

"Decimal."

I return my attention to the little man behind the big desk.

"What. I'm boring you. This relationship. The spark is gone. Magic has died. What."

Rosenblatt speaks too fast, staccato, it's jarring. I close my hand over the bottle of pills in my pocket, and clear my throat.

"Pardon, sir. You were briefing me vis-à-vis the Ukrainians."

"Yeah, so, what. Fucking animals. Eat their young. My point: they get reorganized, that's the kibosh on a fair percent of current and future construction projects. Cost prohibitive. We go back to this Local 79 mess, they'll be expecting health care and thirty-hour work weeks and fuck knows what else on a velvet pillow. Decimal. Have a pistachio. Vibing Dachau over there. Creepier than usual, which is saying a mouthful."

He extends a small ceramic bowl with Hebrew lettering, filled with nuts. I demur. Microbes, human feces, double dippers. Like that fucking bowl of seeds in Indian restaurants.

I get out the Purell™, give a squirt, rub my hands, shaking my head. "Allergic."

"Ha!" Daniel holds his hands aloft, as if describing a marquee. "Decimal's Achilles' heel, revealed. Kryptonite. Mental note. Should you go rogue. Ha."

I smile. I want to take a pill but it's been, tops, twenty minutes. Say, "Pistachios and walnuts. Now you know, Mr. Rosenblatt. So what are we getting at, give somebody a visit in the usual manner?"

Using his Mont Blanc, Rosenblatt scoots a legal-size manila envelope toward me. "Yakiv Shapsko. Emigrated 2000, all the T's crossed there so INS can't lend a hand. He's the instigator. A real *community leader*. The fucking balls. Guy had the nerve to get in on a, need I fuckin tell you, frivolous suit against the city back in '06. Yeah. Ground Zero bullshit."

I get out a fresh pair of surgical gloves, pull them on. Slide out a series of eight-by-ten photos, and four pages of text. The man, husky, military haircut. An address. A couple kids in the mix somewhere, ages seven and five, but their current location and pedigree are hazy. Wife, aged thirty-nine. Another photo.

"Decimal, I don't want to hear a goddamn word about this guy again, ever. Sticks in my craw, you know. Two strikes against him. This union thing, and goddamn personal injury suits. You want to know what made this country bad to do business in? Unions and goddamn personal injury suits. Ask any-fuckin-body. Two big factors. Guy has to go, Decimal."

I nod, replace the materials, rip the gloves off, bin them. "Done."

Rosenblatt does a drumroll on his desk with finger and pen, tappity-tap. He's rather fidgety today. Is he nervous?

"Fantastic. What else we got?"

He glances at an open leather binder. "Staten Island Ferry thing . . . can you believe? Fucking Coast Guard, leaving this clusterfuck in my lap. Huh. Midtown Militia. Clean that up? That's a group effort, a posse thing. Lemme see. LaGuardia deal . . . nope. Transit Authority? What Transit Authority? Fuckin clowns. Oh. How are you for meds?"

"Could use a refill." I say it before I think it, but it's true.

Daniel grins and folds his hands in front of him. How I loathe this man.

"Now. Don't want to waste my valuable time doing the math. We are using the medication as prescribed, right?"

"That's right."

"Not snacking between meals. Nothing like that."

"Nope."

He takes a blank sheet with his office's letterhead, makes a show of unscrewing his pen cap, which he indicates. "Titanium." Wiggles his eyebrows.

"Uh-huh."

He puts a scrawl in the middle of the page, hands it to me.

"You know the protocol. Talk to Andrews—"

"Third floor. I know. It's been six months with this."

Rosenblatt grins again, which is a horrifying sight. He scratches his skull with the aforementioned titanium pen. "Thing is, with you, information retention is not a strong suit. Sometimes I have to repeat myself. This is why we write things down, Decimal. And hence the pills, right?"

He waits, but I blank him, casually apply a little more Purell™. He shifts in his chair.

"So, Dewey, what are we doing?"

"Quieting this Shapsko citizen."

"Correct, but I told you I didn't want to hear another word about that guy. Now get the fuck out of my office, you're killing the plants with your bad energy. Keep those hands clean."

There's a map of the city tattooed on the back of my eyelids. It's two-dimensional, in color, and resembles the MTA's official rendering of the subway, veinlike lines of green, blue, red, yellow, and orange demarcate their respective routes.

This map is always at my disposal.

If you could see this map, the System I speak of would be very clear. It's all there, laid out, alive. Its rules and functions specific, pure (yes, like Purell™), and precise.

When I'm exhausted or overwhelmed, or in that slippery state between sleep and consciousness, my attention is diverted north. I'm a pinball, seeking the center of gravity. North, along a green artery numbered 5, a particular station.

In these moments I'm quite sure that all things/events stem from this location, this place with such a goddamn lovely name. Or perhaps all things/events are headed there, rushing through the green vessel to converge, to come together, at Gun Hill Road.

Nobody owns me but I'm a man of honor, so the late afternoon finds me swallowing a pill across the street from 142 Second Avenue, otherwise known as the Ukrainian Social Hall.

Needless to say, I've cleaned my hands between every cigarette, of which there have been exactly ten.

Minimal foot or vehicle traffic. An electric van with a CDC logo passes by, the occupants in space suits clocking me through mirrored headgear, police lightbar on the roof flashing silent blue and red.

Makes me wonder what the fuck I don't know.

Been here for an hour and a half. To be honest, I'm shocked to find the place still in operation. Suppose it's due to the inordinate amount of Ukrainians in the construction industry, those who stayed behind for the Great Reconstruction.

What a joke.

An orgy of kickbacks, fraud, graft, and a leveling of whatever workers' rights had survived to that date. An avalanche of cash to be had, should you be on the right side of the mountain. Very few were. Very few had stuck around.

A handmade poster on the glass door of the Social Hall proclaims, *Buffet: 11 a.m. to 4 p.m., all you can eat $10,* in Ukrainian Cyrillic.

There's been a sparse but steady trickle of people in and out.

Yet to clock Shapsko so he must still be inside. There's no rear exit.

I've heard good things about the food here, but don't do buffets. Bacteria. The thought of it makes me grab another handful of P and rub the bad away.

Mr. Shapsko was a cinch to locate. His file was short but comprehensive.

Just after my tête-à-tête with the good D.A., I commandeered an "abandoned" vehicle on White Street, a rather nice if scuffed-up Nissan Leaf. Jacking these battery-operated vehicles is an absolute snap, if you know what you're doing.

I then wiped down the interior, scoured my hands, and proceeded to the workplace indicated in Shapsko's file, a contracting company called Odessa Expedited, Inc., at 572 West 26th Street.

I smoked four cigarettes, disinfected, and observed Mr. Shapsko exiting the building, about 12:45 p.m.

I made him easily, although the photo in his file must not have been too recent; he looked to be about fifteen to twenty pounds lighter and had that sunken and drawn look to his face that is common to all post–Valentine's Occurrence New Yorkers, myself included.

Shapsko was accompanied by two white men of similar build, similar haircut, similarly clothed. The trio piled into a '09–'10 Toyota Prius, and at that point I groaned, anticipating a bitch of a tail: these cars were legion, they had been sold en masse at half the sticker price at some point, for reasons unknown to or forgotten by me.

The Prius backed up (illegally) to Eleventh Avenue and headed south. Even as I put the Nissan in gear, two things occurred to me: 1) must clean my dirty hands; and 2) no need to be concerned about losing my target.

New York City had all but emptied over the last year.

Or so it seemed. In actuality, it's at about 10 percent of the population as recorded in early 2011. That's about 800,000 people, counting all boroughs. Nobody knows for sure, impossible to know. Hard to get used to though.

Even prior to the Valentine's Occurrence (which was really a series of coordinated occurrences, plural; I find it irritating and inaccurate to refer to that day as a single event, but when a name sticks it sticks), folks were leaving in droves, especially after the third major economic crash and the free fall of the dollar.

We were ready for the first big crash, more or less ready for the second, but certainly not the third, which was effectively a death knell for the dollar, euro, pound, rupee, and yen.

And then, the Valentine's Occurrence(s). A.k.a. 2/14.

Traffic, at any rate, was light.

Shapsko exits the Ukrainian Hall shortly after 4 p.m., accompanied by five men this time, including the two with whom he had initially come downtown. The group stands near the entrance, engaged in conversation.

At a certain point the whole crew bursts out laughing, and four of the men begin moving in the opposite direction of the Prius. Shapsko waves them off and heads toward his vehicle with another man.

I have a decision or two to make at this point: brace him here with his friend being an unknown quantity, or continue my tail job.

Fuck it; I extinguish cigarette number eleven, wring my hands with the good stuff, and, checking for cars (yeah right, but habits die hard), cross Second Avenue at an angle.

They're both at the Toyota. Shapsko has his keys out.

"Yakiv Shapsko." I pull out my bogus Homeland Security badge. The name on it is Donny Smith.

I'm doing my white people voice, the voice of authority.

Shapsko half turns. He looks amused. His companion moves toward me but Shapsko places his hand on the man's chest.

Hold the badge near the man's face but I already feel like I don't have any control over this situation. Shapsko radiates smart, competent. I would've pegged him as a yahoo.

"Mr. Shapsko, I represent the department of Homeland Security . . ." His friend starts jabbering in Ukrainian but I continue. "And request that you accompany me for questioning."

"Regarding?" Shapsko has this expression like something's funny, which I find annoying. He still rests his bare hand on his companion's chest. The man's denim shirt is dark and can't possibly be clean.

"Regarding matters of national security. That's all I'm authorized to tell you."

The Ukrainian then gives a disarmingly genuine smile. The hair is different, and his nose looks reconstructed, but I feel like I might have met the guy before.

"Am I under arrest?" His English is solid, colored by that proto-Slavic accent.

"Sir, I'm merely asking you to answer some questions, if you'll just accompany me . . ." I like to keep it as professional as possible, but use broad strokes.

"Am I under arrest?" he repeats, as if to a child.

It's a reasonable question, to which I say: "No, but that can be arranged if you'd prefer to go that route."

Jingles his keys. "I do. Have no arrest warrant, I won't go anywhere with you." Almost apologetic like.

His pal is inching toward me. A couple other guys have come out of the hall and are watching the exchange.

This isn't working out. What am I doing? I'm pretty shitty at this direct approach.

"Sir, I need you to understand that I'm characterizing your behavior as uncooperative . . ."

But he's in the car and keying the ignition, his friend scuttling away. Yakiv looks at me from the driver's seat and shrugs. The Toyota pulls off and is up the street before I can organize my thoughts.

I clean the hands. Shit. Now he knows I'm coming. Should have played it NYPD/old-school style, run up on him and hit him. Or hid out in his backseat. Well, had it not been a Prius.

I'm telling you, I'm not particularly smooth. Out of habit I touch the key in my front pocket.

Ah well. Let's do it the easy way.

Ditch the Nissan right there on Second Avenue. Then it's the 6 train uptown to the R at 51st Street, as per the System. Fortunately, the closure of the 23rd, 28th, and 33rd Street stations allow me to do this and remain faithful to System dogma.

Let me explain. Late afternoons, the rules flip: necessary to take number trains and, if need be, transfer then to the lettered ones. It's always good to take the subway versus drive, if you have a choice. It's an eco thing, a hangover tenet from the fossil fuel days.

R train service terminates at Forest Hills, so I figure I'll hoof it to Kew Gardens. Not too familiar with that part of Queens but I will tell you it's nicer than you might think. Or was.

High-rise apartment complexes, a single light on the seventh floor of one building, absolute dead silence.

Ghost-town stuff.

I pop a pill; starting to get a headache . . . realize I'm absolutely starving. Check and make sure my key hasn't slipped out of my pocket . . . nope, still there.

Even in the best of times I imagine one would've had difficulty finding a shop open, but I luck out and come across a BP station that, despite the *NO GAS, ATTENDANT IS ARMED* sign, looks friendly enough.

I trade the terrified Pakistani/Indian/subcontinental Asian man an unopened pack of Lucky Strikes for a log of beef-and-cheese jerky, all he has in the way of foodstuffs. He has at least fifteen large boxes of the jerky. That's good gear to have on hand.

I keep on my way, wondering who buys anything anymore.

I have Shapsko's address down as 12 Mowbray Drive, a very nice mid–twentieth century house, a proper house technically in New York City, which always blows my mind . . . It's modest but charming, the lawn and foliage have grown wild in a not unattractive kind of way. There's a noisy generator in the yard, as well as a dirt bike and a tricycle.

The house's position makes surveillance a bit difficult: I'm forced to loiter across the street in front of an apartment complex, feeling conspicuous. No sign of the Prius, but lights are on in the upper floor.

Before I have time to establish an appropriate spot from which to observe quietly, the porch lights come on. I step backward, quick, into the entryway of the apartment house, stumbling on a loose tile. The entryway, Allah be praised, is unlit.

Iveta Shapsko (née Balodis), aged thirty-nine, Latvian national, height five foot six inches, weight 127 pounds, brown hair, green eyes. I make her easily from across the street, hair pulled back with a stray lock falling across her face, taking the mail out of the box next to the entryway. A small dark-haired boy appears in the doorway, probably Dmitry, the five-year-old, Iveta saying something, pushes him back inside with her, turns and slams the door. The brass knocker bangs twice and the *2* in the *12* is swinging free.

And I am hit in the chest by shock waves from across

the road—communicated in whole to me is Iveta Shapsko's long-standing anger and frustration.

Not knowing how I know this or the source of these feelings but realizing I care, all of this playing out like a set piece, a scene I've seen before, from which nothing good can come . . . My presence here is malevolent, my intentions murky, and the fear of that yawning void from which I access this knowledge propels me out of the vestibule, walking fast and then running, a marble-size obstruction in my throat, sprinting down this tree-lined street in Queens, again into warm rain, but as I bring the back of my hand to my cheek, I think no, not rain, not rain at all.

Because there's a dark thing implanted in the frontal lobe of my brain, ever-present, a cruel sequence of images, profoundly monstrous. It's this: a figure materializes, fades in from black, in a concrete playground attached to a low-income housing project, moving into a metal elevator, moving into a hallway, moving through a door into a silent apartment, into a bedroom, a form beneath a worn sheet. And then the shots, two of them, impossibly loud, and I wake, the reverberation of the shots, and the lunge for the receding shapes. And cut.

Always the same dream.

Iveta triggers something buried in my chest. Do I know her? I can't be sure. Perhaps she's standing in for someone, or something iconic.

Now, it's important to understand that I believe I have had certain aspects of my memory erased while laid up in D.C. What's more, I believe I had false memories implanted. I have no way to prove this, it just feels true. It's a gut thing. As a result, I look at my recollections or dreams with suspicion.

Regarding this dream. My therapist at Walter Reed, Dr. Rosita Lopez, framed it in this way: as I am unable to accept the loss of my wife and daughter while I was deployed, and as a manifestation of my then trendy Post-Traumatic Stress Disorder, I repeatedly visualize an imagined reenactment of the crime committed against my family.

In the view of Dr. Lopez, with her frumpy nylons, her clipboard, and her surreptitious glances at her wristwatch, my acceptance of the realities I face will bring these visions to a close, and banish the imagined assailant from my apprehension, forever.

What I failed to mention to Dr. Lopez is the fact that, should I force my gaze downward in the midst of this recurring brain-film, the imagined assailant is wearing my hands. And shoes.

Due to the 2/14 Occurrence(s), all available written information on any given subject is frozen in mid-sentence, a portal into the era known simply as "Before."

It's fascinating: all the signs of what was to come are right there in the details, this is a truth, despite the mind's desire to revise history through the prism of what is currently known.

Take this bit of trivia from 2011's *CIA World Factbook*:

> *Latvia's economy experienced GDP growth of more than 10 percent per year during 2006–07 but entered a severe recession in 2008 as a result of an unsustainable current account deficit and large debt exposure amid the softening world economy.*

Unsustainable. Softening. What mild, bureaucratically vanilla terms. Words a citizen can acknowledge, shake her head at, what a shame, a tragedy; and continue shopping, working, bench-pressing, consuming, wasting, using, poisoning.

I shut the hardbound volume and return it carefully to my "active" stack, being sure to apply Purell™ afterward.

This stack here? This is material that I keep on hand, relevant to my current situation. I find it informative, comforting, an aspect of my larger project: reorganizing the library's stock in accordance with the antiquated but deeply logical Decimal system.

Somebody's got to do it, man. The internal computer network here having fritzed out, it's nearly impossible to find what you're looking for.

But as I've said, dig: I have my own comprehensive System, the Decimal thing being a piece of the larger puzzle; and therefore I have structure. Otherwise: chaos.

Since I'm doing this on my own, it's slow going. A righteous chore. After four months I'm partway through 000, which is "computer science, information, and general works."

The founding fathers of the Decimal system couldn't have know what a gargantuan amount of material would come to fall under this heading. Especially the subheading "computer science." Jesus. And "general works"? Don't get me friggin started.

Reams of books, numbering in the thousands, stack Dr. Seuss style along the entire stretch of the left-hand wall of the Reading Room. This is my work to date. I reckon I have a year to go on 000, maybe more like two.

It's a safe bet: if the architects of this place knew that a colored man would remain its sole keeper, they would've had coronaries.

This hobby, if it can be called that, has given me an identity as well.

DA Rosenblatt dubbed yours truly "Dewey Decimal" based on my interests, and due to the fact that I can't remember my given name.

The DA says he has my birth records, Social Security card, etc. on file, but I don't want to see these documents, as I don't think I will recognize that person.

Prior to DD I was simply known as "The Librarian," and older acquaintances tend to still call me this. I don't care; I answer to anything. But Dewey Decimal, it's starting to stick.

Tonight the library is dead, which is how I like it.

I crack open a pistachio, make sure it's clean, toss it in my mouth. Add to the bowl I have dedicated for pistachio shells. Every couple of days I disinfect them, and transfer the shells to a sealed baggie for future use. The Scattering of the Shells. I have my rituals, I have my habits.

Since upkeep of these landmarked buildings was transferred to the Parks Department, I don't think I've seen a single ranger, or whatever they call their agents. I'm not so sure there still is a Parks Department, come to think of it, not that it matters.

I assume they've got headquarters in the park, but nobody goes in there. I wonder about the Central Park Zoo, the clock with the animals. Idly I touch my key.

Apparently it's up to me to hold these halls down, which is my distinct honor. Sure, there are countless apartments and lofts, sitting empty and unused, up and down the canyons of Fifth Avenue, Madison, Broadway. Down in Tribeca, northwest to the Meatpacking District, uptown to Central Park West, spaces unclaimed and unprotected.

Some of these once housed the very wealthy, and are extremely opulent. I've seen them. You wouldn't have to be that ambitious to set yourself up in such a place, as many have; but I feel an obligation here.

When I returned to New York after my (illegal, mind you) detention at the Walter Reed Medical Center, then the National Institutes of Health outside Washington, D.C., this place is where I came to rebuild my head, like so many others before me, and I was welcomed.

Not by the staff; that's not what I mean. The very stairwells, the walls, the forests of literature enfolded me, said good to see you back, soldier. Here you'll find rest, and poetry.

In the bosom of the Reading Room I retrieve my kit, lay out my bedroll. Wonder where the mother and child got to, the ones with the hotplate. Wonder if I imagined them. Projected holograms.

Plug my razor into that outlet I noted earlier, find myself cracking a big grin as the blinking yellow charge light appears. Fantastic.

Before sleep, I take a pill and remove my Beretta M9 from its cloth, clean it, load it, etc. The gun feels like an old pair of jeans, conformed to my hands alone. Hands that I now clean as well.

Starting to feel like I'd better be wearing the weapon. Better to have and not need than to be caught out naked.

Always the same dream.

Let's try this again. With a fresh shave and renewed energy, I pull on a surgical mask, walk west to the C train. Exit at 23rd Street. Wearing my gun, got my Purell™, my pills, and of course the key in my front pocket.

Through a tunnel of foul air I cover the few blocks northwest to Odessa Expedited, Inc., confirm Shapsko is on the premises.

Locate his Prius, jack it.

Head out to Kew Gardens.

All this, before 9:30 a.m.

You'll understand that I'm feeling pretty positive as I hit the Queensboro, waved through by a team of army engineers as I press my laminate to the windshield. I've got surgical gloves on as well, so I'm okay with touching the glass in this shit-ass car.

The 59th Street Bridge got lucky: on the occasion of the Occurrence(s), only a small fraction of the planted explosives detonated, leaving the bridge structurally sound.

The associated tramway wasn't so fortunate. A single tram car dangles like a forgotten toy, approximately 250 feet above the East River. Heard it took them three weeks to get the bodies out of that car. Or maybe I made that little tidbit up. Hard to know.

I get on the 495, which I then take to 678, in perfect

accordance with the System, which prescribes odd-even numbered roadway sequences, taking exit 13 SW. In order to keep with the System, I make only left turns (admittedly this takes me a bit out of my way) until I reach Mowbray Drive.

So as to make it a left, I pass the street, pull a U-turn, and backtrack . . . finding myself parked in front of 8 Mowbray, two doors down from the Shapsko household.

Clock says 9:55 a.m.

Tempted to just sit tight and chill till after 11, so I don't run into any unexpected right turns, but I'm concerned the wife will make the vehicle and assume her husband is home.

I remove the surgical gloves and toss them on the floor. Lower the mask. Refresh with Purell™, two times for good measure. Pop the second pill of the morning, and I'm ready.

Today I have a fully System-compatible plan, brutally simple.

Up out of the car (left), noting it's going to be a deadly hot day, goddamn, that smell, nobody around, I proceed straight up the pavement, bypass the Shapsko's, spin one hundred and eighty degrees (left), back to the walkway for number 12 (left), turn up the path and onto the low wooden stoop, I bang the knocker twice, identifying the missing screw that allows for the *2* in *12* to hang akimbo.

I wait. I hear movement inside. I have my Beretta pressed against my left ass cheek. My right hand is free.

The curtain in the window on my left twitches. Keep my head low, hat obscuring my face. I can hear someone on the other side, breathing. Then: "What do you want?" A woman's voice, presumably Iveta. That accent.

I adopt an anxious white person tone, and say in Ukrainian: "Mrs. Shapsko, I am very sorry, but your husband has been in an accident on a job site. They took him to the Armory, he sent me to get you."

Silence from behind the door.

"I'm so sorry to be the bearer of this news but we must hurry. Your husband is injured."

What, is my Ukrainian not convincing? I've been told I sound like a native; even, specifically, a native resident of Kiev as opposed to the south.

Then again, hookers will say anything.

"You are a friend of my husband from where?"

Relief fills my chest; her Ukrainian sucks worse than mine.

"I am a lawyer for Odessa Expedited, and a cousin of his coworker. Please, it's most urgent."

I wait. Is this a typical wifely reaction? Maybe it's a Latvian thing. Hard-ass chicks hail from that ghetto corner of the world. I can practically hear her thinking.

Then: "You can tell my dear *husband*," she spits this word like it's poison, uh-oh, "he can tend his own wounds. While I tend to the care of his child, about whom he seems unconcerned, considering he has not been around more than twice these last four months. You might tell him that, lawyer."

Recalculating. Okay, they're estranged and I am a lawyer. So: "Mrs. Shapsko," I move closer to the door and lower my voice a bit, "the secondary reason I am coming to you is that should his injuries prove severe, or God forbid fatal, you are legally entitled to be the partial beneficiary of any monies resulting from the suit we intend to bring against Odessa Expedited's client. This we should discuss, the status of your relationship or any marital issues being of course not my business and irrelevant to any conversations we might have."

Pretty proud of how that came out. I feel her *really* thinking now.

Wondering how this impacts my overall plan. I add: "But I need your consent to move forward with any litigation, as you are his emergency contact and have de facto power of attorney in this situation."

More breathing. I try to sync my breath to hers. Shit. This has been unexpected. The spouses are separated. Might be a major problem.

There's part of me that finds this to be good news. I squash that aspect of myself, gotta be on point. Anyways, I decide not to abort this mission, yet.

I hear the chain being slid out of its track, and the door comes open. A longish nose, a face that suggests nobility despite the sweatshirt and jeans. Deep green eyes, flickering, indicating that involuntary mental flinch many white people exhibit upon coming face-to-face with a person of color. I have a lifetime's worth of experience with this reaction and I do not take it personally.

Iveta rallies. "The boy is sleeping, just, a . . ." Clearly sorry she opened the door, but I'm already coming in.

With what I hope is a reassuring but concerned expression, I step into the house, Iveta backing up.

I extend my right hand. "Charles Bartosch," I say in English. "I apologize, I assumed you were from the Ukraine."

She accepts my handshake, cool rough hands, glancing past me at the street, takes a step forward to try to steer me backward, saying: "No, it's just that . . ."

I bend her hand back, hard and fast, twist her arm up; she doesn't scream but takes a noisy gulp of air, good girl. Kick the door closed behind me, turn her around, and, forcing her into a kneeling position, I place the Beretta square on the nape of her neck. Her hair is up in a blue bandanna, and it's a lovely neck. I note a medium-large mole an inch below her hairline.

"Shhh. It's okay, it's okay," I tell her.

I'm momentarily dizzy at the reality of being near this woman, but this is the kind of thought hiccup that gets a man killed in such situations, so I promptly back-burner my emotional/empathetic self, nix that shit.

She says a couple things in what I assume is Latvian, a language I don't understand, then in English: "God-DAMNIT, what you want? I'm motherFUCKING stupid. I could tell you weren't Ukraine, this accent is bullshit."

"I've been told different. In fairness, now, I was going for second or third generation."

"Motherfucking thugs. You, Yakiv, all fucking garbage, criminals, why come here? You're not Ukraine, no black guys are coming from Ukraine."

"Yeah, I imagine not."

"My cousin, he comes in here five minutes—if he finds you here you have big problem."

I don't buy that classic for a second.

"Mrs. Shapsko, I don't believe you. I think you're on your own here. Am I right?"

She starts trembling, which I don't like because even though the safety is on, I don't want her to go jerking around and perhaps cause an accident.

Accidents happen. I'm living proof.

Me saying: "Where's your kid, lady?"

Iveta lets out a long, low moan. "Noooo, no, the boy is not here. Please. He's at friend's house. Please."

I push her neck a tad with the gun. "I'm not here to hurt anyone, see? Now you just said your boy was sleeping, so don't try to tell me different. Where is he?"

"No. No." Iveta digs in. Presses her neck against the gun. "You're here for me, I know this, I knew this would come, Yakiv has sent you to kill me, motherfucking coward, because he can't do it for himself. I see what is happening. I won't fight. I won't fight. Please."

Damn. Brave girl.

"I am not going to hurt anyone, all right? I swear to you. Okay, no children. But I need you to do something for me. First, please be still. Hush now."

Iveta is breathing rapidly through her nose and tears have appeared in her eyes. "No. Fuck you. Killer."

This tweaks me. For the second time in twenty-four hours I feel like a situation is sliding out of my control; I'm not accustomed to this sensation.

Feels bad.

"Not here to hurt anyone, Iveta, I'm not a killer but I'll repeat: do what I ask, and we don't involve the kid. Okay by you?" She's quiet. I'm studying that mole. Can't help it, say: "You should get that there mole looked at."

"What?"

"The mole. On your neck. It's, like, discolored. Go to a dermatologist." I feel stupid, she'd have a tough time finding a dermatologist. "Just some advice."

"Are you fucking crazy? You break into this house . . ."

"I didn't break in, let's walk it back. You let me in."

"Liar. Killer. I do nothing for you. Nothing."

"Yes you will, hon. Or we bring out the child. Final offer. Sorry about all this."

She deflates. I adjust my grip on her.

"I'm a very serious man. All I want is to talk now. You talk to me, and I leave."

"What do you want?" She's barely audible.

We're at the foot of the stairs in the foyer. I drag her toward the dumpy living room, she knee-walks the rest of the way. Get her seated in a sky-blue La-Z-Boy.

This is a lot harder facing her. Those emerald peepers laser-beam raw spleen.

"Is your telephone still working? Your landline?"

"No. I have this radio. Like a, um . . . police radio."

I nod. "What's going on with you and Yakiv? I want the whole deal."

"What's going on? But you must know if he sends you here . . ."

"The guy did not send me. Okay? Help me out, what's your situation, the status of your relationship."

"This is private . . ."

"Not right now it's not, and if you don't start dancing with me I'm going upstairs."

"Okay! Okay. This is torture just to speak of, so you are torturing me just now."

"No I'm not. You'll know it if we get down to some torture, which I would be very sad to see happen. But it's always an option, please speed up your narrative here."

Iveta adjusts her bandanna. I sit on a coffee table, the gun still pointed in her direction.

"Yakiv is a dead man to me. A rapist and murderer. I know he will kill me, or send someone like you."

What the fuck is with this hostility? "I've gathered you're not getting along."

She laughs. Minus the amusement. "Not your fucking business. But yes, you could say that. You could say that. I cannot sleep. Every small noise. I'm so afraid for the boy, that he might . . . hurt the boy."

"Why would he want to do that?"

Iveta assesses me. She shakes her head. She's got snot and tear residue on her lip and cheeks but she's no longer crying.

I want to take a pill, I desperately want to disinfect my hands. Nervously I touch my key, but just for a second.

There's a box of Kleenex on the coffee table, and I hand her several. She takes them but doesn't clean herself. This is making me nervous.

"But *why* are you here?" A tear slides down one side of her face.

"You haven't answered my question. If you answer my questions, I might possibly consider answering yours. Why would Yakiv want to harm you, or his own kid?"

"The boy, from another man, another piece of shit."

"Detail noted, but let's stick to my question."

Iveta bobs her head, wipes off the snot with a tissue. "Perhaps you think he is good man. An honorable man. Perhaps you think he will hold up bargain you have together."

"As I've said, I have not been sent by Yakiv, and neither do I know the dude."

She looks at me, taking in my suit, my shoes, my skin. "What are you, black? I can't tell."

Sigh.

After two African American presidents and a Chinese

woman on the moon, can we not yet say we've evolved a "postracial" consciousness? Even as those once-termed "minorities" make up the majority of the population in this country?

Of course not, though this bullshit "postracial" term was popular several years ago. Can you imagine? What a freaking joke.

Well, am I black? Say, "That's off-topic, but I am of mixed racial heritage, and yes, my father was from Trinidad. My mother was of Filipino/Saint Lucian extraction. All this giving a . . . darker tinge to my pigment. Is that helpful?"

I don't know if I'm lying or not, cause I don't recall exactly. But it sounds accurate, and it flows smoothly out of my mouth.

"It is helpful, actually, I tell you why," says Iveta, balling up the Kleenex. "Yakiv hates blacks, South Americans, Chinese . . . he hates all these people, and most of all the black. The only job he might give to black guy, MAYBE, is hired killer, and since you haven't killed me yet and ask all these questions, I'm thinking maybe you don't know my husband. As you say. Giving you money would be very very painful for Yakiv."

I laugh. "That's amusing."

"No, it is not funny. He is like a crazy man about this. I know from this that you cannot possibly be a friend of Yakiv. Impossible. Impossible. Maybe he hired you, but only maybe."

"Been telling you I do not know the man."

"Okay, so then . . . you don't know he is killer. Rapist. Has no . . ." She indicates her forehead, blanking on the word.

"Conscience?"

"That's it. No. He is beyond bad. See. Hates black . . ."

"Yeah, we touched on that."

"Hates women. Hates communist. Hates, hates, hates. Please, I don't understand who you *are*."

Communist? Another word that went out of circulation awhile back, when those governments that had formerly fallen into this category rose to dominant-empire status. What do they call them now? Like China? Benign postcapitalist military dictatorships. There's probably a more elegant term available but I'm not privy to it.

But who am I?

"I'm nobody," I say. "I'm a bad fucking dream. Interested in getting a hold of your husband. And that's all. Do you understand?"

She nods, eyes wide.

Think I'll kick it to her from another angle. "If he has committed crimes, as you say—"

"Many murders, many rapes . . ."

"Yeah, so if that's a fact, I would like to see him treated as a criminal. I promise you. I work for the government."

Iveta drops her eyes. "Is this the truth?"

"Yes, it is," I say, and I'm not quite lying. Technically.

"Then please, if you can take away this gun, it's very frightening for me."

I give this consideration, thinking if I set the thing down somewhere near me and make the mistake of glancing sideways—

Iveta is on me in a heartbeat, she's got a pen or something, going right for my eyes.

I catch her hand and we fall sideways. With her free elbow, she attempts to break the bridge of my nose; my head is slightly averted so she strikes my cheekbone.

Reflexively, I crack her upside the head with my gun. She rolls off me, I didn't knock her out, holding her hand to her temple, blood beginning to flow between her fingers. Head wounds bleed a lot.

Damn, I didn't come here to pistol-whip the woman. Make it right.

"Iveta." I get into a crouching position near her. "Iveta, do you have some, uh, first aid materials? You've got a bit of a cut there."

No response, she grunts and rolls sideways, supporting her head.

I look around the living room. On the sad couch there's bedding, a sheet.

I almost gag, a used fucking sheet, search my pockets for some fresh surgical gloves. Make sure I haven't dropped the key. Pulling the gloves on, I suck it up, grab the material off the couch.

"Iveta. Let me take a look. I have to know you're not going to jump me again, though. Okay?"

"Okay," she says, muffled by the arm covering her mouth.

I take her hand away, there's a shitload of blood, thanks be to Christ I put on the gloves; I apply the sheet and press it to her temple. She blinks at the blood in her right eye. I dab at it as best I can.

We sit like this for a while. I actually have no idea as to what comes next.

"Mama?" A boy's voice, tremulous and scared. Shit. He's in the doorway to the living room now, his mouth an *O*.

I gotta say something.

"Your mother hit her head but she's fine. Go back upstairs. Okay?"

The kid is frozen in place. Iveta shouts something in Latvian and he's gone. I hear a door upstairs slam shut.

"Ma'am," I say, "I apologize for hurting you but you did assault me."

Iveta stares blankly. "You broke into my house with this gun."

"Nope, lady, you very kindly invited me in. Now you're making up shit."

"You say you are government worker."

"I am. Part-time."

She swallows. "Yakiv is also government worker."

Well now. "U.S. government?"

She nods.

"Do tell," I say.

Bleeding under control, we're sitting in the living room, across from one another. I'm in the chair; she's on the couch. I get this notion like we're about to go to the prom.

There's a nervous energy but I dig on it. I like this woman. So much so that I want her to stay okay. I'm watching her for signs of concussion and thus far she looks like she's recovering fine. Keeps pressing the sheet to her head, checking it.

"Hey, yo, listen. Stop doing that, it's clotted, you'll mess it up."

She doesn't respond. I've fetched her a glass of water, from which she takes a long drink. Wipes her mouth with her sleeve.

"Yakiv is—"

"A killer and a rapist, I know."

She shakes her head impatiently. "Mafia, back in Ukraine. Assume he start with running goods, not legal stuff. Guns, drugs. Then it was people. Before this 'Occurrence' . . ."

I nod emphatically. Trying to vibe: skip this part. Everybody has a Valentine's Occurrence story—where were you when, how you *felt*, how you're *feeling* now, etc., etc. I'm not the least bit interested in such touchy-feely nostalgia, and I don't want to hear it.

But Iveta doesn't go there. She continues, "Transport mostly girls, some boys, but mostly girls. For, you know . . ."

Yup, I know. That was a worldwide epidemic.

"Tell them they have job at nice restaurant or hospital, whatever. Then takes away the passport. Puts them in apartment . . ."

"I know what you're describing. Tragic." I say it and mean it.

"Me too, I was one of these girls." Her face flares and she looks at me accusingly. "But I never did anything like that. I was student, trained as nurse, speech therapist you know, I have some skills. He was talking very poorly, like with a stutter. I can fix this. Also, he likes me very much. So I become his girlfriend, and later in Las Vegas we are married. God, he was so drunk. Well, okay, me too."

A wan smile. She takes a Newport out of an open pack on the coffee table. Offers me one.

This is a loopy deal. We're, like, hanging out. I shake my head. "Thanks, but I'm allergic. To menthols."

"Oh. So is it okay if I . . . ?"

"Yes, it doesn't bother me secondhand. Plus, your house."

True this. She fires it up, exhales.

"I should say to you, leave. Why haven't I said leave?"

I shrug. "I have a gun."

"Yes. What is your name?"

"Dewey."

"That's a strange name."

"It's African."

She shrugs. "Dewey, I don't know how you're involved with this, but these people . . ." She trails off.

"Well, I'm a freelancer. I'm not tied to one thing or the other, per se."

"Yes, but in the end we all work for somebody. I should really check on Dmitry. May I go do this?"

"Of course."

Iveta gets up and exits. I scan the room.

Really and truly: the joint is depressing, and is in possession of not one item of interest. Amazing how people choose to live.

I take the opportunity to bust out some Purell™. The only thing that could make this place more depressing would be the presence of a cat.

I hate cats. I really fucking hate cats.

Subdued voices from upstairs.

I take a pill. Have to chill, gotta destress. I can't believe I started thinking about cats. Cats are satanic. Choke on a piece of steak in your apartment alone, and your beloved cat will walk all over your corpse and eat the chunk of meat straight out of your dead throat—

"Dewey, don't move."

Sweet Christ. I'm an idiot.

Iveta is in the doorway, aiming what looks like a Sig Sauer P220 at my head. Naturally.

"Place the pistol on the floor and kick it away."

Goddamnit. I could probably take her out first, but I do as I'm told. I don't want to hurt this woman.

The gun skitters away, under the fake rosewood IKEA entertainment center. I hate anything called an "entertainment center," you just know it can only look shitty. I hate IKEA. It's an inhuman environment, toxic. I wonder about the IKEA in Red Hook, Brooklyn, tomblike, abandoned.

"Stand up slowly."

I start to get up, perhaps a bit too quickly. I'm anxious and unhappy with my performance here.

"Slowly! I said stand up, but do it slowly!" She shouts this, her voice cracking on the "up."

Dmitry peers around her legs. He's wearing a backpack, and holds a largish Reebok sports bag.

They're going to run.

I stand, as slow as I conceivably can. Iveta tells Dmitry something, and he scurries out the front door. Yeah, they're gonna jet.

"I get it," I say. "I won't follow you . . ."

As I'm finishing this sentence, I observe (too late now) that she has shifted her aim to my leg. Without pause, Iveta shoots me in the knee.

Prior to the pain eclipsing everything else, I'm thinking she's got fantastically steady hands. And although she owes me a pair of slacks, I'm thinking I don't intend on holding this incident against her.

I'm looking at that map tattoo on the back of my eyelids. I faintly note external movement, a repetitive sound not unlike the wings of a bird in flight, but this is not important.

The MTA, as it happens, has not one but two stops it calls Gun Hill Road. Both are a snap to get to but I'm talking about the station serviced by probably (some might argue this point) the most reliable train line in the city, the 5 express; because it lets you out right there, the place I go now.

I imagine myself exiting the train, taking the stairs two at a time. I'm out on the street, but pressed somehow, agitated: *Go, go, go*.

If I walked just a bit south, I would in time get to the Botanical Garden. In the past I've found solace in the garden. But I can't go there now. I've got somewhere else to be, something specific to verify.

I head west, toward Woodlawn Cemetery.

The DA is pissed off. NB, even when he's not pissed off he talks too loud, no sense of decorum; what's that condition called? A kind of socially insensitive behavior. What's it called? Sounds like: ass-burgers.

Regardless, I'm compelled to hold the walkie-talkie thingy away from my head whilst Rosenblatt spouts and spiels.

". . . any idea how much a *kneecap*? That kind of technology? Costs the goddamn taxpayer?"

People pay taxes? Quel retro.

I'm laid up in the new VA Medical Center, formerly Mount Sinai, on Madison and 98th Street. Uncomfortable as hell, not because of any pain, I've got an old-looking bag of morphine drip-dropping such bodily concerns away . . .No, it's the fact that I'm in a military medical facility and I'll confess, it's nerve-wracking. Don't like the morphine clouding everything up.

Military hospital.

The last time they had me up in one of these houses of horror I underwent a lot of bad shit, said bad shit causing me huge memory gaps, possible false-memory implants, as well as (I suspect) some sort of physical tracking device, installed deep, near a vital organ I would imagine, as to be undetectable.

I'm aware how this sounds, but I feel it. Back to it: "People still pay taxes?" I talk into the bottom of the thing.

"Very fucking funny. *Citizens* still pay taxes, Decimal. Unlike off-the-grid nonpersons, such as yourself."

That rankles. "I don't appreciate . . . I am not a nonperson."

"Course you are. You don't exist. Officially. Appear in no public record. I like you that way, Decimal. YOU like you that way. Makes you employable, more interesting. You once told me you like that, make up your goddamn mind."

"I prefer to think of myself an individual who keeps a low profile."

"Ah, I see. Well, it's going to be tough, keeping a low profile. Should you have to go through any metal detectors. With that new knee of yours. Six million–dollar man. Cue you: this is where you say, thank you, sir."

Six million dollars? What's that all about? Say, "Thank you, Dan."

"Thank you, SIR."

"Thank you, Sir Dan."

"The fuck? I medevac you? Out of some outhouse in frigging *Queens*? Helicopters and the whole nine? Talk about fucking inconvenience. Lucky I think on my feet. Otherwise: questions. Questions we don't want asked, see? Decimal, you are the massive fuck-up here. Not me."

"Sir, if you'll allow—"

"No, I won't. We don't do families. Not classy. Are you classy?"

"I'm nothing if not classy, sir."

"So I had thought. So I had THOUGHT. You dress well. For a freakin vagrant. Kids? Women? No fly. Nyet, nein, nope, no way, never. We do mano a mano. Or not at all. Do you think I'm talking out of my ass?"

Sure I do, but say: "No sir. Perhaps I misread the finer points of the assignment, as the file contained photos and information that included an address, family—"

"No, no, no. I should take you off this. Right away. But I like you. There's trust here. It's a chemistry thing. Maybe I'm losing it. Going soft."

"Sir, the direct approach, it's a difficult prospect, as the subject strikes me as an intelligent and well-trained—"

"Your observations. On *character*, are noted. But I do not give a shit. Two things: you stay on this job. Wrap it up. One. Two: you do not approach Miss Balodis under any circumstances."

I frown at this. Who? Oh right, that's the maiden name . . . "Shapsko."

"Yeah, right, that's right. Miss Shapsko, the wife, her, any kids. I'm issuing a restraining order. Got it?"

"Yes sir."

Maybe it's the dope making things cloudy, but something seems strange about the mention of this woman's unmarried name. But I can't trace this, much less complete a thought.

"Decimal?"

"Yeah, still here."

"Okay. So the job is the same. It's the man of the house you want. Now. When you're up and running again. Counting on you. Nobody else appropriate for this thing."

"Understood." Another thought. "Sir, not to offend, but I get the sense that you might have seen the need to put a tail on me."

"Oh? One: I'm insulted. And B: what would lead you to this fucking conclusion?"

"Found me awful quick. You know, out in Queens."

The D.A. sniffs. "Yours, Decimal, is not to fucking question your superiors. Your guardian fucking angels. I won't be insulted by a shitbird like you. Clear?"

"Crystalline."

"This a secure line?"

I have a look over at the doctor or nurse or whatever he is, Asian guy, upon whose walkie I'm speaking.

Dude makes like he's studying a chart, as if it's the most fascinating thing he's ever laid peepers on. I've been holding the device a foot from my head, there's no way he hasn't heard everything.

"Yup," I tell the DA. The doctor glances my way, I toss him a wink.

"Good. Good. Just do like you like to do best and keep that low profile low."

"Roger that."

"Roger who?"

"Always wanted to say that on a CB."

"Decimal: heal the fuck up, get this thing done, no muss no fuss, and then fuck back off to your books."

DA terminates the call. I hand the device back to the doc.

"That was my boss."

The doc, like I said an Asian kid, Korean or something, sticks out his lower lip. "Not my concern."

I'm getting sleepy, things slowing down. "Doc, am I going to make it? Give it to me straight." Voice it like last-stages-of-throat-cancer, don't know why. Gallows humor.

The guy looks at me askance, like I'm an idiot. Thought he'd appreciate it, oh well.

"You've had knee replacement surgery. You're fine. But I would think upwards of six months' physical therapy . . ."

"Nah, I'm good."

Doc offers me a tight expression, something in the strained-smile family. "It's not optional. You want to walk upright again?"

I shrug. Major correction: morphine is nice. "Tell me all about my new knee, doc."

"State of the art. Ceramic and titanium."

That's way rich. I laugh at that.

"What aspect of this is funny?" The doc is blinking his eyes rapidly. Seems annoyed.

"Titanium . . . My boss, he's got this pen . . . it's a goddamn *pen*, mind you, see, so . . . man always waving it around . . ." I get that far and forget why it was funny.

"You should be taking this very seriously," says the doc. "You're aware that you were given priority, placed directly at the head of the line. We're completely understaffed, and have more cases than we can handle as it is."

Touchy.

"Additionally, I don't like doing procedures on somebody without a complete set of records. It's dangerous. I'm aware there's a political dimension to all this; frankly, though, I grow weary of this secretive stuff. Creates an uncomfortably large margin for error, and isn't fair to other patients who might be forced to wait while you types get treated. Please express this to your employer, if you would."

Prickly.

"And if that's the same Daniel Rosenblatt who

brought so many lawsuits against this facility in the past, please let him know that he's responsible for the firing of at least two good physicians, known personally to me. The man used to stand down in the lobby, handing out his card. Unbelievable."

Am I my brother's keeper? "Gosh, doc," I say. "Well, can't speak to that, but let me at least say thanks."

The doctor mumbles something. Cranky guy.

I say, "Also, if you've got a moment and I'm not pushing my luck, I could use a couple aspirin. For my PTSD. Maybe we could cuddle too. Give me a safe space to cry it out."

Doc rolls his eyes and shoves off. Godspeed, doc.

He's all right, that fellow, despite the hair up his ass. I appreciate everything he's done for me, really I do.

Not 100 percent on what that is, but if the DA is to be believed, it was expensive.

I'm in a private room. Deluxe, like. I lie still, listening to hushed conversations outside, full-throated screaming from some point beyond that.

I'm in a military hospital.

Military hospital equals fear and loss, no control, factors unknown but certainly nothing good. Fuzzy details, but the fear is there.

Designer viruses, spores, airborne bio-nano weaponry. Probes, man.

I gotta pee. Thinking about probes will do that.

I ease the IV out of the vein in my hand. Haul myself up and almost nosedive into the floor. It's like having one leg. I do some painful hopping.

Note my belongings, clothing, check the pants for the key, okay, laminate, plus, amazingly, my gun (you should have seen me back in Queens before I passed out, doused in blood, right knee decimated, probably in shock, dislocating my arm to retrieve the pistol from under that evil-ass "entertainment center"), all of it in a clear plastic sack, hanging off a peg in a cubbyhole.

A box of surgical gloves. Could it be Christmas?

Note the Purell™ dispenser on the wall; you have to love that. Want one for the library.

I'm ready to hit the dispenser, ready to cleanse. And then I'm ready to bounce.

My first mistake was stealing a wheelchair as opposed to a crutch or something, more or less broadcasting my defenselessness to all and sundry.

Not to mention the freaking monster of a hill around 96th Street. I'm vibing Special Olympics, with a strong emphasis on the "special."

My second and far more serious mistake, but related to the first, was reckoning I'd take Fifth Avenue all the way down to the library.

Fifth Avenue, of course, borders the park. Park entrances are festooned with yellow police tape. Crosstown motorways are blockaded with piles of rock, log, and garbage.

Within lies who knows what kind of darkness.

And here's me, grunting and straining, surgical mask and hat, in a goddamn wheelchair, half-stoned on the dope, essentially announcing "easy target" to anything that might emerge from the unknowable hole that is the park.

My gun, needless to say, is in my lap. I'm trying to remember how many bullets might remain in the clip. Can't scare up this information. I don't think I shot at anybody recently but my powers of recall are not running at their full potential.

Did I mention this?

It's quiet. Bad quiet. I'm on the east side of Fifth, as

far away from the park as possible. There's no question I'm being observed.

Even at night, the air here is more melting plastic than oxygen. That smell, always that smell. The Stench.

I need to pause and take a pill, they're in my jacket pocket, but I don't want to stop moving. Thanks be to Christ I pulled on a pair of those gloves prior to exiting the hospital, the thought of touching these wheels with my naked hands raises my gorge.

I'm at 73rd Street, arms trembling, biting my tongue with the effort of pushing my carcass up the slight incline that is Fifth Avenue.

I hear a *thunk*, and a brick appears in my path.

As I try to digest this, *wham*, something whacks my right wheel, missing my hand by inches. Something else whistles by my head. I get the general thrust of things.

To my left is some overgrown shrubbery near the entryway to a once-fancy apartment house, I size it up. Register a sharp sting in my upper arm as something tags me there, thankfully something on the smaller side. Time to move.

Upend myself, tilting the chair west and dumping my body into the brush, my weight crushing the small branches, and I land behind the shrubs.

A deluge of projectiles—brick fragments, shale, bits of tile. I attempt to shield my head and lie flat. As my bad knee hits the earth I nearly black out and most likely give an involuntary scream, though I can't be sure. I feel warmth in my crotch and am dismayed to realize that I've pissed my pants. Just a touch.

Whizz, bang, chunks strike the wall behind me, bouncing off the air-conditioning units, smashing holes in the windows, one of which gives and shatters completely, and in due course I'm covered in and framed by glass shards.

My gun is in hand. Hope it's still loaded, so tough to keep track of such things.

The shower of debris is slackening and I take this opportunity to make sure my key is still with me, check, and to work my pill bottle out of my pocket, trying not to stab myself with a spear of broken glass. Praise be the bottle didn't fall out, I get the top off one-handed in a much-practiced maneuver, angle my head back, and coax two down my gullet.

Downpour of crap comes to a stop. I cock the hammer on the Beretta. Voices.

It's Portuguese. I'm sure of this, though I'm hardly fluent. At least four individuals. Brazilian Portuguese at that, which I certainly don't understand. Sounds like an argument. Probably beefing as to who comes over to check me out. They do have reason to be concerned.

Or maybe it's like that Chinese thing where they always sound like they're chewing each other out.

I'm no longer concerned. Not really.

The voices cease, or at least fall below audibility. I'm trying to gauge if I can get up. I run a checklist of my motor functions, which comes up at about 50 percent. As in, I cannot rely on the lower half of my body. Not super great. On ten, I will make the most of my arms, will rise up if possible and bring what I got.

I'm not hearing anything. Count to ten.

In one big push-up I rise from the brush, trying to put my weight on my good knee . . .

A short, stocky man freezes halfway across the avenue, all I clock is a wispy mustache. I don't even think about it, I pull off a shot and he folds up on himself and slow-motion face-plants on the asphalt.

Guess he got the short straw.

I don't recall hearing the shot, which is odd, but now there's general shouting across the street. Apparently I've made an impression.

I do understand the word "arma" . . . register the sound of a group of people crashing through the brush, perhaps retreating, falling back into the inky wilds of Central Park.

Wait till all is quiet again. I retrieve my hat, then very very gingerly come to a full standing position . . . I surmise that the least bit of pressure on my bad knee might cause me to lose consciousness and I can't afford that now.

My beeper has been obliterated . . . oops. No way for the DA to page me now. Que sera.

Guy prostrate in the street, in supplication. I can see his upper back rising and falling, not dead, not yet. His navy-blue T-shirt reads *Jeter* and the number 2, a bit of Yankees swag.

I'm a Mets fan. Or was. Go fuck yourself: you try growing up a biracial Mets fan in the South Bronx.

I see no weapon, save a large bread knife that must have been in his hand, and is now about ten feet out of his reach. I do see an exit wound, lower back, blood rapidly dying his T-shirt black.

A freaking bread knife . . . that's pretty bleak. Even for a punk scavenger.

Can I walk? Hardly. Dragging my useless leg, I hop-skip in his direction.

The wheelchair is trashed. Goddamnit. It wasn't a perfect solution, but what now?

Approaching the prone figure, I feel a tug in my stomach. Nothing I can articulate. Something feels wrong, off. It's easier to sit back down and kind of shuffle over to him on my ass; I do so with a growing sense of dread.

I arrive at his side. His respiration is choppy and erratic. I have to know, so I roll him over. Not a short man, not at all. More like a kid. Seventeen, tops, and probably younger. His features are fairly wrecked, but he's presenting all the facial aspects of Down syndrome.

He blinks at me, blood gathering at his mouth, bubbling out his nose. It's a straight-up gut shot, square in the lower abdomen, absolutely zero hope, but I drop my weapon, knock his head sideways so he doesn't choke on his own fluids, and apply direct pressure.

Just a kid, just a big kid. A handicapped kid.

I'm talking, saying, "I'm so sorry. I am so sorry. I didn't know who . . . A hospital, I can get you to a hospital. No problem. Kid, you have to look at me . . ."

But he's elsewhere, watching from some distant point. Blood is running freely from his nose. Oh Jesus, I think . . . I think he's trying to smile at me.

"You gotta believe that I would not have hurt you. Had I known . . ."

Yeah, he's smiling at me, which is more than I can bear . . . I'm pressing at the wound hard but he's bleeding out, a small pond of blood has formed, flowing freely from the exit wound in his back.

Now I'm just babbling, with no reason to believe he understands my rap. "Hey, kid, you like baseball? Speak

English? Nod if you're with me. You gotta stay with me. Okay?"

His expression doesn't change, though his jaw slackens a bit. I feel him fading. I press his abdomen harder.

"No, listen. We're going to get you help. Listen. I have a story. When I was a kid, younger than you, my dad took me to the old Yankee Stadium. Not that crappy new one that got hit. The old one they tore down. Listen. So he gets me sitting down and gives me two bucks for popcorn and candy. Are you listening?"

I shake him and his eyes roll around to meet mine for a moment, then come unfocused again.

"Listen. Back when they had Rick Cerone pitching, he was pretty great, people don't talk enough about Rick. They're playing the Red Sox, a big game. Maybe it was the Series, I don't know. So I'm watching the game . . . Listen to me."

I slap his cheek. Again his head lolls back in my direction. The movement of his chest is growing harder to detect.

"I'm watching the game. It's a good game. You know. And then I think I haven't seen my dad in a while. I start wondering, hey, where'd he get to? Listen."

I push his face again and this time he doesn't respond at all. I keep talking.

"So I check the men's room. I'm looking at all the lines at the concession stands. Can't find him anywhere. Are you listening?"

Blood has soaked my left pant leg. I keep talking.

"So before I know it, the game's over. Everybody's leaving. Smells like beer and mustard and sweat, I remember that. It's like a crush of people, just so many people, laughing and fighting and shouting, and I'm starting to get scared, right? I'm calling for my dad. Walking around and around the stadium. Just calling for him."

I know this kid is dead. I keep talking.

"So eventually, what can I do, I leave. I walk home, it's a long ways but I know where to go and I walk home. To my mom's, that is. It's dark when I get there and my mom, she's furious, asks me why I ran away from Dad. Because it was a Sunday, and he had me on the weekends. She's talking about how I should respect my dad more, and I keep trying to explain, Mom, Mom . . ."

The kid is very much dead. I release his gut and pull myself up.

I'm standing, wobbly, but upright.

Commence hopping south.

Feel like I need to allow the story to wrap itself up, I'm learning things, because this is not an active memory I have, and yet here I am describing it, so I continue speaking quietly. It's like automatic writing.

I'm observing myself, listening, saying: "Mom. It wasn't my fault. She's not hearing me. Says I have to go over to his house, that's where I sleep Sundays, she has company coming and it's his night. I know there's no arguing with her. I go. Walk to my dad's project. I buzz him and buzz him and nobody answers. So I sleep in Claremont Park, on a bench. They gave us these crappy little beach towels with the Yankees logo at the game, I use that as a pillow. Turns out: Dad went to a bar and forgot about me. So . . ."

I stumble over a rut in the sidewalk. I'm in serious pain, but I press forward, the key in my fist.

"Needless to say, from that point on I was a Mets fan."

My brain goes empty. Is that it? I wait for a postscript. Nope, c'est fini. Well, how's that for a gun-to-the-soft-palette bummer of a story. I was hoping for a less heavy-handed wrap-up.

See, I'm suspicious of such yarns; could all be bullshit, false memory. It lists too far toward the weepy side. Overly pat somehow.

So I'm thinking: probably bullshit. But man, the detail. These elaborate lies I tell myself. To what fucking end?

Regardless. I attain the bottom of the park. To my left, what remains of the Plaza. On the right: the former Apple computer store, which appears structurally viable, despite the ordinance I know to have been detonated on the lower level.

Presently I limp by Bergdorf Goodman. It's all winter shit in the windows, cream-colored Prada ski suits, wool capes, and whatnot. They had this up in mid-Feburary? It's no wonder the displays are intact. Who wants to boost this kind of gear in the middle of a heat wave?

Even my sweat feels filthy. I pause to strip off my gloves and hit the Purell™, which praise Yahweh is still to be found in my pocket.

Having done so, I slip on another pair. I love that initial powdery sensation of these gloves, it whispers "clean," if you listen close. And I do.

Pass a night crew doing some kind of shit, a manhole open, yellow tape, floodlights, big red tent with a zipper, people moon-walking about in those creepy-ass space suits. Not the white suits, the orange ones with that biohazard logo on the back.

I stumble-slide forward, pulling my mask back on.

And as I pass St. Thomas it occurs to me: 2/14, they left the churches alone. They didn't hit the churches. To my knowledge, only the mosque across from the Freedom Tower sustained damage, and best guess that was due to its proximity to a major target.

And at this point I've gotten better at walking, calibrating my step to favor my as-yet-undamaged leg. Making little adjustments.

Focus on the System, which has a way forward for everything.

Six months of physical therapy my caramel ass.

Get that prickly feeling around the backside of Rockefeller Center.

I'm on the east side of Fifth, and I sidestep into the northernmost doorway of bombed-out Saks & Company. Heart rate up a touch, even accounting for the physical exertion.

Take a look back up the avenue, casual like.

Yup. A black Lincoln Navigator idles a block down, between 49th and 50th, in front of St. Patrick's. Blue parking lights on. Trying to make like they weren't tailing me.

I tell myself I'm processing shit paranoid. But I rarely believe me. Consider possible moves. Decide to hang back a bit, stay put. Plus I don't mind the breather. My leg smarts like a bastard. Feel for a cigarette, I have none. I keep forgetting . . .

My gun is holstered, but I'm a happier man for wearing it. I wanna scrub up but I got the gloves and wanna keep them on in case I need to bolt. Not like I'd make it a yard before my new knee snapped like a stale pretzel stick.

Another look. The Navigator loitering. I make out tinted windows, therefore can't get a peep in.

Considering this. Lincoln Navis are strictly VIP rides. Engine conversion to battery way cost-prohibitive for just any Joe Schmoe. Celebrity, status whips. Not much changed in that respect since the bling-bling hip hop self-projections of the pre-Occurrence(s) world.

Guys I knew growing up would posture-pimp, renting a Navi or a Lexus or an Escalade for special occasions, along with the obligatory assortment of neighborhood chicas, some of whom were available for rent as well.

Drive the beast around town, bass in the back rattling folks' windows. Shoot a video, YouTube it, smoke a blunt, and bullshit to your friends. Short-term large living.

Come morning, you're back to your slog at Best Buy or Applebee's.

Brothers would razz me because I favored that "think-y" Brooklyn/Queens stuff. Tribe Called Quest, Mos. Uppity fag shit. Despite the fact that I wore Skulls colors, which, honestly, never felt like me.

Except for the violence. Was always good at that part.

Imagine the ridicule, had they found me digging Stravinsky. Mahler. Ornette Coleman. King Tubby. Fela. Good stuff out of my dad's record collection. Even now I can smell the vinyl and the faint mildew of the jacket covers.

Snap out of it. Back to the Lincoln. Thinking: the only other stratum of society who still rocked these tanks would be government. This sets off a whole new round of unbalanced speculation.

Can't just stand here like a soft bitch. I use the brass doors to push off, direct myself south like a gentleman taking the air. In no hurry.

Don't have to turn around to sense the Navi's approach. My gun hand twitches, cowboy style. Ready for whatever.

The vehicle pulls parallel and paces me. Provocative . . . I can't be hobbling more than three miles an hour.

Face front, keep on hiking. I don't acknowledge the Lincoln. Again my hand spasms a bit. Amber alert.

Can't help it, I glance sideways. Smoked-out glass, revealing nothing.

Me, primed for a tussle, a bracing, a shoot-out, what have you.

I guess they lose interest or opt out, cause the driver gases it and they pull away from me, kind of lazy like.

Smoked-out rear windows as well. Look though: the plates—red, white, and blue. Diplomatic plates.

I watch the SUV as it hangs a right onto East 47th Street.

Realize I've been holding my breath.

Maybe it's the paranoia that's keeping my ass alive.

Dig the two heavily muscled men sitting astride one of the marble lions that bookend the library steps, facing one another.

I've been watching them from the recessed entryway of the former Nat Sherman tobacco shop (later some useless chain clothing store) for about six minutes. Northwest corner of 42nd and Fifth Avenue.

I'm exhausted and just want to lie down. How much of my life, in hours and days, have I wasted watching other people from a concealed vantage point?

The brawny lads seem to be speaking quietly and sharing a cigarette, up there on the lion. Feels like I'm watching the beginning of a high-concept guy-on-guy porno, that part you'd fast-forward through to get to the action.

Fuck this, I decide to move in on them. No disguising the fact that I'm walking wounded. I have my gun at my side.

Now: if I'd started with a full magazine, I should have fourteen rounds to go. The Down syndrome kid, his guileless smile, pop up at me, I knock them back and bury them.

The boys are watching me, as I do my funky limp their way. Aware that I'm podcasting Halloween-scary, a bloody black apparition in half a suit.

The fellows dismount, not particularly graceful in their movements. My goon radar is spiking. Goon city.

And I make them for Baltic/Slavic twenty yards away. Hope that doesn't sound racist, you can just see it. Tell me I'm wrong.

These people are the new goombahs, nouveau-Guido, used to be the Italians. And they dress accordingly.

The boys fall into bouncer positions, seemingly a natural bearing for this body type. Legs a touch wide, arms folded.

"Good evening!" calls one of them. Yeah, I hear Eastern Europe.

I hobble up and stop, about ten feet shy of the heavies, scope them. One has a shiny black T-shirt with a massive Armani logo, the other is rocking one of those miserable Ed Hardy pieces favored by this class of character, an off-white number with crisscrossing stitching up the sides, and a pair of yakuza-style "sleeves," renderings of a koi pond, colorful fish, and shit. Both are wearing linen trousers and man-sandals.

I get the douche-chills.

"Gentlemen," I greet them, hoping they don't register the quotation marks.

"Beautiful place to come home," says the talker, the one in the Armani tee. Like overfriendly. He tilts his head in the direction of the library. "To live in such a place is to feel like a king. What do they call this place?"

"It's a library."

Armani pouts his lips and nods, admiring the Beaux-Arts façade, which still looks pretty clean. "Very good. If they are making a condo inside, I buy one. I come talk to you, huh?" He grins at me.

"Don't hold your breath on the condo. And I don't own the place, I'm just the custodian."

Armani is nodding. Custodian is a big-boy word so I doubt if he got me, but he's nodding all the same. "It is Mr. Decimal?"

"Indeed it is."

"Perhaps you are hurt? Wishing to sit?" He glances at my leg, the bandages, my filthy pissed-in slacks, of which one leg has been cut off at the thigh. I see him note the gun, by which he is unfazed.

"I'm good here," I say. "Your manners are impeccable, and I appreciate that. Now what can I do for you cowpokes?"

Ed Hardy is looking me up and down, slowly. His eyes have that unoccupied look of heavies the world over. They alight on my gun and stay there. He's got a jailhouse tattoo on his neck, some gang scrawl, the Jack of Spades.

"Some discussion, some talk. More comfortable inside?" Armani half bows in a lead-the-way gesture.

"It's a public building. You gents might be more comfortable inside, but I'm fine just where I am. What say we talk here?" In truth I'm aching to sit, but I want these thugs on their way. I cross my arms casually, Beretta in hand.

"Okay. No problems. Guns, no need for guns," says Armani.

"What can I do for you?" I repeat. I'm too tired, really. I need to wrap this up.

Armani's ingratiating veneer slides a bit. "Our boss, he likes to speak to you."

"And who is your boss?"

"Mr. Yakiv Shapsko."

"Uh-huh. And he wants to discuss . . ."

Armani lifts his shoulders and drops them. "Business. What else?"

I nod. "Okay, I'm open to that. Tomorrow morning would work best for me."

The men exchange looks.

"Mr. Shapsko makes suggestion, meeting right away. We take you to him now. Okay?"

I absorb both of them. Honestly, I don't want to be a snob, I certainly do similar errands on occasion, but there's this subspecies that's just so specific. These guys fall into that category.

From past experience I can guesstimate that I don't exactly have a choice about how this plays out. I'm not up to further static. Say, "Look, boys. At least let me change my pants. As you can see, I'm not presentable and I don't want to disturb you or your boss's finely honed aesthetic sensibilities. If I may."

Again the boys share a glance. It's a hair tense. Armani is working his jaw. "Stepan, he is going with you."

"Guys, I'm not a flight risk. Neither you two nor your boss does much in the way of scaring me. I'll go wherever, I don't have anything better to do."

Armani, who I'm sure would love to have at me, is marshalling his cool. "Stepan, he is going with you," says the big man again.

I shrug, put my gun in my waistband, and start up the stairs. It's not easy. "Fine, Stepan, please do follow me."

Armani, in Ukrainian, says to Stepan: "Hurry this up, help the nigger walk."

"Yeah, Stepan," I echo in their native tongue, "help this nigger walk." Throw them off a little.

They don't seem particularly impressed by my lingual skills.

Stepan offers his forearm, the koi warped by his ridiculous musculature. A lesser man would have gagged on his cologne, but I keep it together and take his arm like Scarlett O'Hara.

"You're too kind," I continue in Ukrainian. "Hey, I dig Hardy's gear. It's got that edge." Stepan won't look at me, so I keep talking. "Cousin, in general I just gotta say, I like what you're working with. The big guns here. Since David Barton went under, I imagine you have a fantastically well-appointed home gym."

These guys must be under strict orders and/or truly fear their master. Because their intense desire to beat me into carpaccio is thicker in the air than my man Stepan's cologne.

Which is saying something.

Superflu descended like the motherfucking wrath of God, Old Testament style.

H1N1? That stepchild had been the viral equivalent of *Ishtar*. A big raspberry of a bomb, the failed punch line, all talk and no walk.

Put folks off guard.

But Big Bad Mother Nature learns from her mistakes, makes adjustments, and comes roaring back with an improved model. Those who knew said if you dug the Superflu virus under a microscope, you could watch the bastard mutate, right there before you eyes.

It was perfect, in every respect. And like a snowflake, each and every individual virus had its very own unique design and symmetry. Constantly shifting.

In North America, it's thought that about two million people lost their lives to this pandemic. Even with all our modern medicine, inoculations, etc.

That slightly beats out the Spanish Flu of 1918, given the current world population. No joke.

Course, me, I'd had the secret shot. The one that never went into production. So as the bodies stacked higher and higher, all I had to contend with was a mild case of the sniffles.

Gliding now down Ninth Avenue.

This far west? You can smell the Hudson, even above the Stench. The tainted water level is high, about a meter below the edge of the road. And rising. It's just a matter of time.

As we arrive, I gather the Maritime Hotel on Ninth Avenue and 16th Street is not what it once was, which is to say that it is apparently no longer a hotel. More like a private entertainment facility.

The first indicator my brain didn't identify right away. I'm folded into the cramped backseat of a late-model Ford Volt as the distinctive building comes into view, and I'm thinking something's funky.

As we pull into the former bike lane and come to stop at the curb, it hits me: all the lights are on. They must have a serious generator, industrial kind of gear.

Dude in some sort of fancy burgundy Mao jacket opens the door for Armani (never got his name), who turns and flips down the seat.

"Mr. Decimal. Let's go."

I'm climbing out, obviously not fast enough what with the knee, because Armani grabs my upper arm and gives me a jerk . . . I almost do a face-plant, which would have been embarrassing because we have a potential audience; the mezzanine-level terrace, formerly a nightclub or a sushi place or some shit, is hopping.

Thick with white men drinking cocktails and uniformly slender white or Asian women doling them out. Rice paper lanterns adorn the balcony, and I hear the muted throb of that kind of crappy electronic music to be found only in settings such as these. I spy a waterfall.

The vibe is strictly late-twentieth century designer hotel, and my inner douche-o-meter is pinned hard right.

Mao jacket slides into the car and is off, taking the corner at 16th with a slight screech of the tires. Valet parking?

I have a few questions but Stepan grips the back of my neck, and together with Armani they're hustling our party toward the entrance. This is the largest grouping of people I've seen in the city since the Occurrence(s), outside of a construction site. Clearly I'm out of the loop.

Back at the library, I had been allowed to change, then I was stripped of my gun, my Purell™. They studied my laminate for ages. They took issue with my key, I kept telling them it was just a goddamn key, and eventually they let me hang on to it. I slipped it into my new pants pocket, front right of course.

And it took a lot of talking to convince the men to allow me to retain my pills.

"It's not a freaking cyanide capsule, guys. I have a real . . ."

In the end Stepan simply popped one. We all sat around for five minutes and after nothing happened, they tossed the vial back to me and we split. By that time they'd chilled out, such that they even let me do my thing with the pistachio shells without asking what the fuck I was up to.

The atrium of the Maritime is flanked by two Mao-jacketed robots who nod at my big buddies and don't seem to notice me. I'm hustled up a set of stairs, which would be an impossible act of athleticism on my part without a little help from my friends.

Ridiculously, that ancient folk song pops unbidden into my head and lodges there.

I get by with a little help from my friends
I get high with a little help from my friends

But that's all I can remember of it, so it just loops.

Into the crowded lobby, and all at once I'm engulfed in the kind of crowd scene I had thought long gone. I feel dizzy and nauseous, I lose depth perception. The joint assaults me with color and sound. The wall of body heat is sickening, and thankfully I am propelled through and past it with dispatch by the twin heavies, who steer me into an alcove featuring a wall of elevators.

Surely these can't be in operation . . . Armani inserts a keycard into a metal slot, above which are the words, *Penthouse Level, Private.*

"Guys . . ." Surely we can't be . . . An elevator door which bears a plate proclaiming the same sentiment slides open, and I'm being forced in its direction. I dig in with my feet; my wingers slide on the marble and I am treated to a blast of pain up my bad leg. "Guys, I don't do elevators. I'm serious. I have a medical condition."

"Let's go, Mr. Decimal," Armani is saying.

"Listen, I'm not trying to be difficult, I just can't do . . ."

Stepan puts me in a headlock, cutting off my windpipe, good Lord does this guy ever want to see me die, I shouldn't have played it so snarky. He hauls me like a sack of sand into the mirrored closet that is the elevator.

This is the part where I press the button. Metal elevator. Hallway. Door.

These thought-bubbles drift by, out of context.

I'm trying to communicate my inability to breathe by poking gently at Stepan's thorax. Armani slides the keycard into a panel on the wall and hits the single button. Oh protect me, Jesus, the doors whisper closed.

The grip on my blowhole slackens and I'm sucking oxygen again, the four-way mirror showing an infinite regress, multiple still lifes of me plus gorillas.

I look awful. My hat is askew and my nappy head is in need of grooming. In general I look like a pair of trashed leather slouch boots. Everything hangs off me, my sport jacket, my flesh.

The goons seem disengaged and stare at nothing. The cologne fog is almost visible, I suck at the compromised air through my mouth.

"I just . . . It's not a phobia. I have negative associations . . ."

I'm breathing wrong. Feel my extremities tingling, my throat tightening. I start counting backward from ten. I touch the key for strength. I can't believe I got coerced into a goddamn elevator ride. I fumble for a pill, tip one back.

But nothing's happening. I sense no movement.

I'm getting ready to share my assessment of the situation with the Power Twins, but before I'm able the door slides open, revealing a gigantic, low-lit space into which I am pushed.

There's a party going on here as well, though nothing like what's happening downstairs.

High ceilings, track lights. Couples and small groupings of well-heeled-looking peeps converse quietly here and there. Modelesque girls and boys in kimonos orbit the room, bearing trays with hors d'oeuvres and drinks. The furniture, although dated, looks expensive and inviting. The art is an impressive mash-up of Japanese wall hangings, suits of armor, a Kandinsky, a couple Hoppers, some Dutch master stuff, and a smaller Rodin statue. And that's just what I see immediately.

Multiple wall-mounted plasma-screen TVs play old soundless World Cup footage, probably from 2010. I hear Miles Davis, *Kind of Blue* if I'm not mistaken, piped in by unseen speakers. A few heads turn and take us in, then return to their conversations.

I'm led through the room and down a hallway, herringbone wood floors covered with Oriental runners.

On the walls are jazz/Harlem Renaissance memorabilia, a photo of Langston Hughes framed with what I imagine to be a poem in his handwriting, a playbill of Orson Welles's all-black production of *Macbeth*, a photograph of Billie Holiday mounted with a lipstick-smeared cocktail napkin, Miles Davis and John Coltrane in conversation accompanied by scribbles of musical notation with the words *So What* at the top. And so on.

We arrive at another door, this one looks to be modified as there is no handle on the exterior, only another key card slot and a button.

"Hands on the wall," says Armani, spinning me to face it.

I do as I'm told, careful to avoid the framed bric-a-brac. As they frisk me for the second time I believe I'm looking at an eight-by-eleven poster advertising a show at the Savoy in March of 1934, featuring the Chick Webb Orchestra with vocalist Ella Fitzgerald. *Apollo champion and songbird of Harlem!*

"Fellows, you know I'm not armed. Stepan here watched me get dressed, for Christ's sake."

Armani's patting down my calves and doesn't respond. I'm wearing my very last viable suit, a seersucker with blue stripes, complemented by a white shirt and blue tie, and my usual brown porkpie hat.

The suit is okay for the current season but I'm going to need to work out something else for the colder months.

Assuming I can keep myself alive.

Armani stands and nods to Stepan, who presses the button with his bratwurst of a thumb.

Presently, Yakiv Shapsko opens the door. Scans me. "Is he unarmed?" he asks the boys in Ukrainian, smiling, not taking his eyes off yours truly.

They respond in the affirmative.

Yakiv looks like he just came from work . . . He's got on a pair of Dickies, with a cheap dress shirt and tie. He has a napkin from Popeyes tucked in his collar.

Popeyes. Jesus. Must be the one on 14th Street, the last low-class chicken hut standing. Grew up on the stuff. I shiver inside.

He extends his hand. I accept it. Greasy. Oh for some sweet Purell™.

"Mr. Decimal, just finishing up dinner. Please, come."

We enter what appears to be a high-ceilinged conference room. Full wall of windows to my right, looking toward the water and the anemic lights of New Jersey. A glass table, smoke colored.

At the head of the table is a MacBook Pro from the last year of its production, a large Styrofoam cup with a straw, and a small box of chicken debris. But that's not what I notice first.

On the far wall is a massive, I'm talking something like twelve-by-fifteen feet, medieval tapestry I know very well. If it's not the original, I have to take my hat off to the artist who rendered such an amazing reproduction.

It's a work called *The Unicorn Is in Captivity and No Longer Dead*. It was made somewhere in the area of 1495–1505.

Yakiv follows my gaze. "Yes, real thing. Thought best to hang on to it rather than see it stolen or damaged. Never know."

When I was a kid, it hung at a place called the Cloisters up in Fort Washington. A memory: we went there on some school trip. Chicks dig unicorns, at least they did in the 1980s.

If I have the story right, John Rockefeller bought this piece and its six companion tapestries in 1922 from some nobility in France . . . Later on, the series was moved to the Metropolitan Museum of Art.

I can only nod. "Just hope you didn't get any chicken on it."

Yakiv laughs in a relaxed way, and removes the napkin. Once again I feel the profound need for Purell™.

"No, not this time. I usually try to eat better but . . . busy day."

In his native language, Yakiv tells Stepan and Armani to remove the garbage, and themselves. He asks about the ID. Authentic, says Stepan.

As the flunkies proceed cleaning up, I say in Ukrainian: "I see that you're also a fan of the Harlem Renaissance period." He registers mild surprise. I continue: "I'm nearly fluent so if you're more comfortable we can speak your language."

Yakiv raises his eyebrows.

"I had forgotten," he says in English. "But I think of this English as my native tongue now."

"Fine," I say.

"No, I am a collector, I . . . inherit many things. I like many kinds of art. But Mr. Decimal, I do wonder . . ." He pauses as the big boys exit without a backward glance. "Sit," he says, sitting himself at the head of the table, indicating a chair next to him. Aeron office chairs.

Yakiv clasps his hands and looks out the window for a bit. I desperately want to disinfect. Consider asking if he has Purell™. Decide against it.

The man cuts a decent profile; he's got a strong jaw, is going gray, and at one point wore earrings.

Then: "Tell me what I'm missing. With respect to your methods."

"How do you mean . . . ?"

"Well," he laughs, and spreads his hands, "first you approach me cold, on the street, and present bogus Homeland Security ID . . ."

"I work for Homeland Security, the ID is not bogus." I know it's futile; I have the sense that I'm being completely outclassed here.

"Please, Mr. Decimal. Less than half minute on the phone with Washington, I determine this is not true. Homeland Security only exists like theory now."

Grasping at straws, I try: "That's of course protocol. If I'm in the field, it's standard procedure to deny any knowledge—"

Yakiv waggles his hand dismissively. "Come on. Not worth our time to be like this."

I shrug. "You've been misinformed."

"No, I have not," says Yakiv. "But there's frustration I do have; I have yet to figure out who you actually are, and for whom you operate. It's a frustration."

"Your sources are probably—"

"My sources, impeccable. They occupy very highest level of government both in this country and elsewhere. How is it that you speak Ukrainian?"

The truth is? I don't remember. My theory is I had several languages downloaded into my brain at the NIH. But I say, "Took a night course. It's a hobby kind of thing."

Yakiv blinks at me. "That's your answer?"

"Yes."

"Did you have Ukrainian girlfriend or wife?"

"No."

"Who takes Ukrainian-language class?"

"Guys like me."

"Okay then: why do you assault my wife and child in my home, for no clear reason?"

My turn to blink. "Poor planning."

"Can you elaborate on this?"

"Poor planning, poor execution. You had proved uncooperative, so I took a different approach—"

Yakiv smacks his hands down on the table, hard, but doesn't modulate his voice a bit. "Please don't be insulting. Listen to me: I know you aren't working for federal government, or foreign government as far as I can tell. You might be insane, but I know you're not this lone operator. By the way: thanks for not damaging my car. I like this car."

I don't respond. I think that's best for the moment.

"For one: you were evacuated from my former home via military helicopter. You were treated at military facility, and allowed to simply walk away when it pleases you. The operation you have was extremely expensive one, and any medical files on you, if they exist, have been destroyed. This is difficult, to make an organization on your own, Mr. Decimal."

Yakiv opens his computer.

"Now, we pulled prints off Nissan that you ditched day before yesterday, plus mask and gloves in my car."

I'm wracking my brain; was I really that fucking stupid? Apparently.

"I know you're careful. All we got was single partial thumbprint off of ignition wire housing in Nissan. And some partials off driver's door handle in this Prius. Nobody's perfect. So from this, we are able to trace you . . ."

My stomach is churning. This is suddenly a nightmare. I don't want to know. Yakiv turns the screen toward me. I'm fondling my key.

There, on the screen, I'm looking at a younger, even more haunted-looking version of myself with a bald head and multiple facial lacerations.

The Mac's resolution is painfully high-def.

"To National Institutes of Health. Where you were known as John Doe. This is annoying. *Mr. Decimal*, of course this is an alias, or some kind of joke about your current residence . . ." He pauses, perhaps expecting me to chime in. I don't. "At any rate. According to their files you were initially admitted to Walter Reed several years back, you have symptoms of this Post-Traumatic Stress Disorder, having been in active branch of the military, stationed at unknown location. They don't specify which branch, but having checked with all of them, your records could not be located.

"Main symptoms being 'extensive memory loss, disturbed sleep, paranoid episodes' . . . blah blah blah. You were classified 'nonfunctional' and transferred to NIH for participate in some sort of trial study cofunded by feds, plus private insurance like BlueCross/BlueShield, and drug company Pfizer. The nature or result of the study, this is not outlined. There is only one reference to this study that could be located. And no record of release, or any subsequent actions for you."

He slaps the laptop closed.

"This kind of information blackout, again, is very difficult to achieve. And expensive. Especially military records. So."

I drum my fingers on the table and smile apologetically. Thinking: things to be thankful for. The bruisers at NIH shot me up with a host of experimental drugs, one or two of which wound up being the heretofore-mentioned Superflu inoculation, which never made it to the general public. Hence my continued presence here on God's green earth.

Things to be thankful for. Or perhaps that was the worst of all possible tortures the good doctors could conceivably subject me to. Depends on how you look at it.

But Yakiv continues, "And yet, here you are. This city laminate appears to be authentic, Class 1, like mine, essentially allows us freedom, this movement anywhere."

"Yup. I'm a first-class citizen."

"So by elimination, I move forward, assume you work for this city in some capacity. Am I right?"

I examine my fingernails.

"That's okay. I don't need confirmation from you. I think I have this much figured out. Work for the city, or you are making work for one of my competitors. Which I very much doubt, as we have their organizations under close observation."

Suddenly and inappropriately, I feel very much alone. And with respect to my loyalties, where do they lie?

I might not like Rosenblatt personally, but he has certainly taken care of me when things have gone awry. On the other hand, his motivation for that is self-serving, so he doesn't get in trouble, and these precarious situations only ever come about at his behest.

And he keeps me stocked, in the medication department.

How did I meet DA Rosenblatt? I simply don't remember.

"Mr. Decimal. In what context did you learn Ukrainian?"

See above. I don't remember. "I told you, continuing education. Call me a dabbler."

"A what?"

"A dabbler. You know, a little bit of this, a little bit of that. I just yearn to learn. Know what I'm saying?"

Yakiv looks at me. Taps his fingers on the glass. Rotates his chair 180 degrees, facing the priceless unicorn.

"I am wondering what my," he pauses to cough, "what my beloved wife had to say for herself. Or what she may have told you, related to me or activities of my business."

"What makes you think she told me anything at all?"

"Because I know my wife."

"I don't do marital stuff. I don't get involved. That's a black hole, man."

Yakiv spins back around, slow. "Then what do you do? That's the, uh, crux of the question here. What do you do, Mr. Decimal? What is your line of work?"

"I'm a librarian."

"Well, you've chosen perfect place to live. You know, I try to keep my organization as, what is it, civil as possible."

"Is that so?"

"Oh, absolutely. I don't care what impressions you may have about me or my business, but let me give you example. Let's take this situation here. You, attempting to, I don't know what, abduct me? Interrogate me? Harm me some way? Then bringing a firearm into my former home, with my wife and young child present, making threats, terrifying them . . ."

"If I might, and I'm not debating any of this, when you sum it all up it was in fact your wife who shot me, not the other way around. With her own firearm."

"She was well within rights to do so and you know this. Were you in her place you would have done same thing, or worse, no? My wife, you should be aware, was in Latvian NAF, also involved with NATO activities in Kosovo, 1999."

Don't know what the NAF is, I'm embarrassed to admit, but like I said the woman had a steady arm.

Yakiv continues: "So she has assimilated, this is okay, but is hardly, what do you say, your average American housewife. But listen to me now. Wishing as I do to understand your motive and employer, or employers, I could, just for example, torture you."

"Yes, I can imagine that we're headed down that road."

Yakiv holds up a hand. "But listen to me. I tell you now, this is not how I conduct affairs. Torture, this is for old Soviet Union, and also now for you Americans. Am I wrong?"

"Are we discussing politics now? Listen, I don't go in for torture. But that's only because it gets you bad information, not because I give a shit. Everybody knows that, it's a short-sighted practice."

"I agree with you, 100 percent. So we're what, pragmatic. We talk things through."

"Yup, that's what we're doing."

"And I indulge you in the sense that whoever you are and whoever you are making work for, I don't particularly mind. Because you have independent nature, would this be fair to say?"

"Fair to say. What's your point?"

"I'm willing to overlook this . . . unwillingness to give identity of your employers. That's fine. So all that is past, and all is forgiven. Let's begin again with . . . what, a clean slate is what you say."

"Sure. What is your point, Mr. Shapsko?"

Again he shifts his gaze out the window. A helicopter is moving low across the water, spotlights on. There's always a helicopter.

"Are you a married man?"

This gives me a jolt. Unbidden, I see a woman's mouth, teeth exposed, as she laughs at something, then turns away.

"No . . . I was."

"So you know how it is, with marriage. Life. Things go wrong, things happen, little shifts, little slides, and suddenly, everything is being fucked. Just the way it works. Do you agree?"

"Yes, I do."

"Sometimes things can be fixed, sometimes not so simple."

I nod. Disturbed by the image of the teeth, imperfect teeth, human teeth, deeply familiar teeth. Laughing, turning away.

"In my case I am at an impasse with my wife Iveta."

As a bonus, I see another set of teeth, much smaller and less evenly spaced. One molar is loose; I've tied some dental floss around it and I give it jerk, out comes the tooth, out of a child's mouth.

If these are implants, what cruelty.

"Kids . . ." I don't know if I've said it aloud.

Yakiv is still looking out the window. He gives a little shrug. "Kids, they came with the whole package. Not mine, um, biologically. Legally, yes. I'm not concerned with these boys. The eldest, he is living with Iveta's sister now, in London. Who, incidentally, is literally prostitute. The sister, I mean."

"Huh. How shocking. And I'm sure you know nothing about that kind of business."

Yakiv belches silently into his fist. I smell chicken grease, and that's nasty. "Don't know what you mean. I run a construction firm. Anyway. Haven't heard from this boy in a very long time. As for youngest kid, well . . ." He looks at me again. Lifts and drops a shoulder. "So, in simple terms, conflict with my wife has been reaching point where there is no acceptable solution."

"There's always divorce, man." Listen to Dewey Decimal, the marriage counselor.

He shakes his head. "Regrettably, Iveta won't allow this. Besides, it wouldn't solve this big problem."

"Shame when it gets ugly."

Yakiv laughs at that. "Ugly puts it mildly. Which leads me to this: whatever these mysterious people pay you, I pay you twice over."

Huh. I say, "For . . . ?"

"Feel free to lie to me, increase price. I don't care."

I'm not happy with the direction this is heading. "And . . . although I'm getting the general drift . . . what exactly are you proposing to pay me for?"

Leaning back and placing both hands palms down on the table, Yakiv Shapsko adopts a regretful look. Says: "I am asking you to eliminate my wife, Iveta Shapsko."

Outside of the projects, properly named the Gun Hill Houses. They can give them whatever names they want, they can number them, call them "Houses," or use the word "Residence" or "Estate," it doesn't matter; it's the projects. Everybody knows what that means.

There is a set of conditions that comes with the projects, a set of circumstances. Cheerless and same-y tales of the have-nots or the lost-it-alls. A singular architecture that communicates a code every citizen is hard-wired to decipher: those who live within possess less human value than those who live without.

Outside the projects, even the garbage strewn around the playground is straight-up cliché. Empty bottles of Olde English malt liquor, Cheetos bags, chicken bones, a stray toddler-size Reebok.

Note all of this. Disregard it.

Enter the building. All surfaces are subway-car metallic magic, impervious to Sharpies, spray paint.

Enter the elevator to a cloud of piss and beer. Enter without fear. Push the correct button. None of this is unfamiliar.

Exit the elevator, follow the hallway to the correct door. Take out the key.

Savor this moment. Everything begins now. Enter when ready.

In the pink bathroom I take a blue pentagon-shaped pill. It lodges in my throat for a second, I have that momentary panic. I swallow again and my throat muscles behave properly.

My mouth feels dusty, arid.

Go to wash my hands, using bottled water and hotel soap. The soap only makes things worse. One of those shell-shaped jobs that's more perfumed cocoa butter than anything else.

I dry them, hard. I scrape at them, looking at the bowl of potpourri on top of the toilet.

I avoid the mirror.

Exiting the bathroom, I reenter the conference room.

"Can I sleep on it?" I ask Yakiv, who hasn't moved a muscle.

"No. I'm afraid not. Now that I've put this to you, you either accept job or you don't leave. Makes it simple."

"It strikes me . . ." I say, walking to the window, looking for a balcony not too far down. It's a desperate thought. Nothing but flat wall with a slight slope. "It strikes me that you have a seemingly endless pool of thugs who qualify for a job like this. Why not just use them?"

Yakiv is shaking his head. "No. This cannot be internal. I need this buffer. You're perfect positioned. You assaulted my wife once already. No connection with me."

"Uh-huh. So how about the monkeys who hauled me

in? They know exactly where they took me and can certainly spill on you should they choose to."

"These men have already been, what, dispatched. I select them in the first place because they are breaking our code. Both foremen, extorting lower-level workers. Sex with employees' wives and girlfriends. Stepan is homosexual, so in this case sex with male employees. Beneath our contempt. Best they be forgotten."

I nod. "Sure."

Yakiv dips his head, gives a rueful look. "You think I'm callous? You should know my wife. She'd cut her son's throat if she could gain from it. Her ability to lie, this, this is unparalleled. Her training . . . this is a vicious, evil person. If I've ever encountered truly evil human being, this is her."

And yet . . . she went for my knee. An armed stranger in her home and she goes for my knee.

I consider the unicorn. Such a beautiful picture. How can something be that old?

So why not a head-shot, Iveta? Doesn't it simply make it more difficult for her, the fact that I remain alive? Rather: that I was allowed to live.

Shapsko sighs. "I don't hold ill will toward Iveta. It is not personal in this sense, I want you to understand. I don't believe in, how do you express it, *bad seed* idea. You should have seen conditions from which she came. Raped by her father and stepbrother. Her mother, a heroin addict and prostitute, blames Iveta for every hardship . . . even blames her for these rapes. For stealing her husband. Then she seeks new life in military. Witnesses incredible, incredible brutality in Kosovo. Is taken by Serbian warlord. Branko Jokanovic. Heard of him?"

I shake my head. Sounds like the dude with the paint shop. What was his name?

Yakiv waves it away, not important.

"Well, the Americans did have two million-dollar reward out on his head. Branko Jokanovic. Some horrible stuff, this guy was responsible for. Anyway, Iveta was of course brutalized, knocked around, yeah? Yet again. And in time sold, essentially, to me."

I wonder how much one pays for a white woman like that. I wonder what old Yakiv was up to in that part of the world.

"And I suppose you were down there, a Ukrainian 'businessman' in Kosovo, giving out Gatorade and free hugs."

Yakiv gives a horsey snort. "Free hugs! You're a smart guy. Yeah. You know, I make sure everybody has what they need. Same as now. NATO too you know, I don't take sides in these conflicts. Who can fucking figure this out? It's all local stuff, settling of these old scores. Like high school kind of thing. Or like: your grandfather killed the goat of my grandfather. I was much younger of course . . . Do you mind if I ask, where do you see combat? Perhaps you were down there?"

Where was I? I don't remember where I was. It was really hot and shitty. Smelled like burning tires, gas, cardamom, goats . . .

"Nope, that Kosovo business was just slightly before my time," I say, adding, "As for my deployment, that's classified." I wink at him. "Need-to-know type stuff."

Yakiv tosses his head back. "Ha! *Need to know*! You're funny, seriously. Okay, Mr. Need to Know. I'm sure you're this real American hero."

"Oh hell yeah," I say.

"I have no doubt. Well, as they say: I thank you for your service!" He slaps his thigh. "What a great country, really. All this ridiculous worship of military, stupid Hollywood talk, *the ultimate sacrifice* . . . It's all big movie or video game to you Americans." Laughing. He's cracking himself up over here.

"Yeah, well, we're all just a bunch of monkeys. Cartoons. Cattle. That what I hear you saying?"

The man wipes away a tear, has another brief fit.

I say, "Listen, man. No arguments about your general reasoning. Just remember, though, I get sensitive when I feel like I'm getting laughed at."

Fucking guy doesn't even register that. Fishes around in his pants, pulls out a handkerchief, blows his nose, from which I instinctively flinch.

"Pardon me. No offense intended. Back to Iveta. So this Serbian man, this warlord Branko, he was her first husband. He was in with all these guys—Ratko Mladić, Radovan Karadžić. We are thinking maybe he is working, here in New York—under assumed identity, of course . . . Actually, I am pretty positive I know exactly where he is, but I'm not interested in either revenge or this reward. It's known fact that international and domestic American law enforcement will be moving on him, and soon. Well."

Yakiv wipes his mouth with a Popeyes napkin. Lord, give me Purell™.

"But I won't bother you with further details. Better not knowing them, actually." Rubs his face, all trace of humor gone now. The energy in the room shifts. He says, "So you see. She is what she needs to be. Iveta. Her nature . . ."

Yakiv vibes tired, and older. I look back out the window. Thinking I gotta scare up some smarts, this is a crazy stupid situation. A serious pickle, really. How did this all get rolling? Oh yeah, the DA.

"I take no pleasure in this business," he says. "It saddens me greatly. I tried, I cannot begin telling you . . ."

Another helicopter, low over the water. I watch the Ukrainian's reflection. I might as well talk straight up, and gamble on where that lands me.

"See," I say, "here's my problem. My problem is that I'm looking at this story from several different angles. Conflicting."

I see him smile in the window. "So, my wife says some things, concerning me, and you find them . . . compelling. I see."

"No, I didn't say that. I'm hearing a lot of definite bullshit, and a lot of stuff about which I don't know what to think, from several corners. I'm having difficulty sorting out the good information from the bad. And I have no reason to believe that anybody is giving me the straight deal."

"Mr. Decimal, pardon this directness, but what does it matter who says what about who? We're all, what. We're all sinners here. If the price is right, isn't this deciding factor?"

I sigh. People never fail to disappoint me. Sell me short. I sit back down. "I gotta say, for a smart guy, seemingly, you badly misjudge my character."

Yakiv shakes his head, still smiling. "Well, I didn't mean to, uh—"

"No, listen, you're by no means alone. Happens a lot. The assumption that I don't have my own internal moral code over here."

Yakiv is nodding sagely, like he's right there with me. "Of course."

"I mean, I don't just go running around town switching teams at the drop of a hat, wasting people willy-nilly, you dig me?"

He winces. "*Wasting* people? This is very crude. I don't use this kind of term. People waste themselves when they don't do like they were born to do. And you talk about teams, as if this were football match? No, no. Life is not like this. Life is gray. Like you."

"Like me? Don't follow you."

"Well, are you 100 percent black man? Or are you 100 percent white?"

Please. "That is a stupid-ass metaphor, my friend. You're trying too hard. Know the limits of your command of the English language."

He laughs at that. "Okay, but you see my point."

"Not really. Yeah, yeah, gray areas, so what?"

Yakiv lifts his shoulders and exhales. "All right, let me simplify things for you then."

"By all means."

He holds up his right thumb. "One the one hand: you do this job for me, you get to walk with your life, plus good deal of money. Within reason." Then the left thumb: "On the other hand: you don't do this job, and you get nothing. And you are certainly not walking away. Understand?"

He sits there, eyebrows raised, giving me the double thumbs-up sign. Like the Fonz, I think inappropriately, given the gravity of things here.

Me: "No gray areas when you put it like that."

"Do you understand?" he repeats.

"I understand," I tell the Ukrainian.
Cause what else do you say?

The shaking doesn't start until I actually hit pavement on West 16th Street. When it does, I nearly fumble my new briefcase. Jesus, how anyone can bear the levitating coffin known as an elevator?

I point my trembling gimp toward Eighth Avenue, hoping I can find a respectable place to collapse, unseen by the car service drivers who line the street, the battered Town Cars, uniformly black—man, I wonder what it must cost to convert a monster like a Town Car to battery cell or solar, must be a serious chunk of change. Like a Navigator. Pretty much the same engine, most people don't know that.

I wonder if the C train is operational. Thinking maybe I don't want to run into military personnel with what I'm carrying, and my freaky fritzed-out aura. I zombie-swerve eastward. Just want to be home.

In the briefcase:

—a polymer 9mm Sig Sauer SP2022, plus fifty extra rounds and a silencer. Traceable apparently to one Branko Jokanovic, don't ask me how.
—a thin folder containing information relevant to Iveta Shapsko and her possible location, which I have yet to look at.
—night-vision goggles.
—a Canon digital camera.
—a ziplock of string cheese, and some kind of

fucked-up yak jerky the crazy Ukrainian insisted
I take, "in case you get hungry."

Am I really that goddamn emaciated? Why is everyone so concerned with my diet? Next they'll be sifting through my poop.

I make Eighth Avenue, and the C/E station looks dark. I'm shaking so hard I sit down on the curb. Wait for it to pass. Feel for the key, yes. Feel for cigarettes, nope. Sometimes I forget to keep smoking.

The air is a blanket of toxins.

I pop a pill.

The briefcase, which is equipped with a three-digit combination lock, isn't the only new accessory bestowed on me this evening.

I inspect my new ankle monitor, affixed neat and snug to my bad leg. I've been tethered. Reckon these are tamper-proof so I don't bother playing around with it.

I seem to remember my dad had one at some point. Probably after the second time he beat down my mother. House arrest. I recall having to run to the corner to buy him beer. Before he legged it back to Trinidad, bracelet and all.

If you could only see me now, Pop. I'm a big shot. Lady-killer. On the curb in a summer suit, shaking, shaking, gripping a tan faux-leather briefcase. The night is young, and I'm king of this city. Yes, if I could just see you now, Pop. I got a Swiss buddy named Sig I'd simply love you to meet.

I'm wallowing in this kind of pointless tough-think, or I'm too spaced out by my painful leg. Either way, I don't notice the vehicle creeping up Eighth Avenue, an electric Army Aggressor, until I'm hit in the face by 120 watts of spotlight.

"Hey, hey, totally not necessary, people!"

I do my utmost to scramble to my feet, blinded and handicapped as I am. A megaphone crackles and an amplified voice addresses me and anybody else within a ten-block radius.

"*Hold it there. Interlock your fingers behind your head*."

I do as I'm told, I'm not a complete idiot. "Be cool!" I shout. "I'm one of the good guys, all right? Just be fucking cool."

I can't see much as the light is in my face, but I'm starting to adjust. A pair of doors slam almost in unison, I'm approached by two MPs, one hangs back, cradling an HK machine pistol. The other comes toward me, saying, "Keep those hands where they are. Where's you ID?"

He's a kid, maybe twenty. Freckles, probably a redhead under that helmet. I tell him: "Front left-hand suit coat pocket. Sorry: your right, my left."

"Sir, are you carrying needles or any sharp objects I might need to be aware of?"

Jesus, what is this . . . ? "No, son, it's just a laminate. Careful with those plastic edges, though, they can be sharp."

He gives me a here's-a-smart-guy look, but I'm serious, I've cut myself more than once on those laminates. Just trying to be helpful.

"I'm going to put my hand in your pocket and get out your ID at this time, sir. Please do not move."

"No problem, you'll see shortly that I do in fact work for the city. Just be cool."

The kid gingerly withdraws my ID from my suit jacket. Guy with the HK is chewing gum, looks bored.

Freckles holds my ID up to the light, squints at it. Looks at me. Looks back at the ID. "Mr. Dewey Decimal?"

"That's me."

He calls back to his buddy: "Can you check the list for a Decimal, Dewey, ID . . . Ready?"

"Just a sec . . . Yeah," calls an unseen man in the vehicle.

"ID number 4-7-9-alpha-golf-november-yankee-charlie."

"Stand by."

We do. It's awkward. More for them than me. Freckles thumbs the edge of my laminate, whistles tunelessly for a couple seconds, stops. His bare hands . . . I'm gonna have to disinfect that ID card. Kid sneaks a glance at me a couple times.

His pal with the big gun wears headphones; the engine on the Aggressor is silent and I can make out snippets of Jay-Z, a throwback to the world I once knew well. A beat to which the boy with the machine pistol bobs his head slightly.

To break it up, I ask Freckles: "Do you serve, son?"

Kid shakes his head. Yeah, I guess he'd be a bit young.

Presently, the fellow in the truck comes back with: "ID is good, and, uh, we have a message? Unclassified, quote: *It's Rosenblatt, WT mother F? Contact me via shortwave a.s.a.p., this unit has frequency, etc*. Unquote."

I sigh. I recall my pager, crushed to dust in the bushes somewhere on the Upper East Side.

"Gents, can I be so bold as to ask for the use of your

radio?" Freckles hands me my ID. I take it with two fingers. "And kindly chill the lights out, I'm as tan as I need to be."

It's coming up on three in the morning as I gimp-limp up the marble steps past the twin lions, briefcase in tow. Home sweet home. I'm going to eat this yak jerky, maybe the string cheese, and collapse.

Christ, what a long-ass goddamn day.

The DA was pissed. His usual state. Nothing new there. Why wouldn't I respond to his multiple pages? Dealt with that.

Was I aware that I'd permanently screwed my chances of walking normally ever again? This secondhand from my doc. No I had not been aware of this, but thank you for the heads-up.

The lean, it gives me character.

Was I some kind of smart-ass? Yes, I was.

I enter the library, gladly accepting its cold embrace. Pull the flashlight out of its nook near the door, fire it up.

Agents from the DA's office had tailed me as far as the Maritime, and Rosenblatt knew I'd been nabbed, and in contact with Shapsko. What the hell was going on?

This was far more complex to dance to, but I made it work. My play, as related to the DA, had been thus: I had described myself as a small-time operator: veteran, thief, mercenary, and jack-of-all-trades. Throwing myself on Shapsko's mercy, and offering my services in any capacity.

Far from being angered by my aborted break-in at his

former home in Queens, and subsequent collision with his wife, Shapsko was impressed I had the wherewithal to track him down and tail him undetected. He was further impressed that I survived the encounter with his wife Iveta, about whom he didn't seem to be too concerned; and that I obviously had sufficient government contacts to somehow arrange for a medevac.

Yakiv had a job for me, which was "sensitive." I was to meet him tomorrow, privately, to discuss details at his office on West 26th Street. If I didn't show, Shapsko had said, he would find me and kill me.

So, in short, Shapsko had bought my flimsy line of bullshit. My relief knew no bounds, I told Rosenblatt, who then asked if I thought he gave a shit about that?

I told the goodly DA that my plan, then, was to use this opportunity to whack Shapsko in an intimate setting, as this evening in the hotel had not been ideal; should I have attempted anything untoward, the Ukrainian's men would have gotten to me within seconds.

And unbelievably, incredibly, DA Rosenblatt bought my flimsy line of bullshit. Of course, he made me squirm a bit and crowed on and on about my inability to do anything in a straight line, but in the end he bought it.

Because he wanted to buy it.

And he reiterated his warning concerning Iveta: this woman is a no-go zone. I was not to seek her out, I was not to come within one hundred yards of her, ever ever never again, no, no way, no how.

This seemed redundant, as for all the DA knew I had no need to involve Iveta, but I didn't comment. Don't think I'm missing the fact that it's now twice he's gone out of his way to make protective noises about the woman, despite his total lack of ethics and usual disregard for collateral damage.

Now I rub my forearm and examine the rising red bump. It looks innocuous enough, mosquito-bite minor. But I don't dig it, not for a nanosecond.

This was the big negative that came of my conversation with the district attorney. I'd lost the pager? No problem. He had insisted, rather, that I be electronically tagged. This way he could provide backup if I was abducted, etc. It was for his peace of mind, and for my own safety. His exact words.

And best of all, my new friends, the strapping young soldiers in my company back on Eighth Avenue, had the necessary equipment to do it, right there on the spot. The machine looked like one of those old label-makers. I used to label everything in my room when I was a kid. Even my little fish tank: *goldfish*. Lest I forget.

Little scraps of a life I assume is mine, patchy as hell.

Anyhow. Freckles had administered it. *Pop*: a little pinch, and I had a state-of-the-art circa 2011 microchip buried in my arm.

Fantastic.

As I move into the belly of the library now, I consider the two GPS units affixed to my person. Who monitors them? How much information do they impart? What kind of equipment does one use to do so? Between Shapsko's outfit and the DA's office/military, who has the more impressive gear?

I picture Shapsko's moodily lit outpost as staffed by sexy Eastern European females of dark hair and complexion, clad in black catsuits, matte black earpieces, with a holographic wall of 3-D renderings of my precise position, posture, heart rate, and ever-shifting moods.

Likewise, I envision the DA/military spread as a shoddy, fluorescent, plasterboard affair, some temporary office setup, hastily assembled, with shitty metal chairs and disgruntled, unattractive demotees peering at a blinking white blip on a black field like the earliest generation of video games, about whose location they can only make vague approximations.

I bet you that over at Shapsko's joint they have some sort of complex rotating computer model of—

Hold it. I freeze midstep and am brought smack back to my surroundings. I direct the light left to right, and up and down the stairwell.

Where are my pistachio shells?

See: whenever word spreads (and it spreads fast) that I'm on a job, all squatters know to avoid this place, as if whatever nefarious shit I'm up to creates a field of bad energy that repels them. It's weird but it's true. I don't mind; I'd much rather be alone at any given time, though I tolerate them when they're around. It's a public building. It's my public building. So whenever I start a job, I know I need to be extra careful.

And in case you haven't caught on to this yet, I have a System. The System is made up of Maps, Rituals, and Patterns that I like to repeat in certain circumstances. Also Tokens, which I guess you might say in my case is the physical pill bottle, the key of course, and the bottle of Purrel™. Plus my hat.

Rituals are classified as Safety, Hygienic, and Other (or Miscellaneous, if you prefer, but Other is a less ungainly word, I reckon).

One of the Safety Rituals is the Scattering of the

Shells. I collect them in my shell bowl and cast them about as I leave the library without fail, always and only on the third set of steps. And I clean them up nightly with my trusty Dustbuster. Should I notice some crushed shells upon my return home, I might expect to find visitors upstairs, and be prepared accordingly.

In this case I'm not seeing any shells yet, anywhere. Broken or otherwise. I play the flashlight up and down. Correction: since the lights are off in the whole building I'm going more by sound than sight, and I have not heard the familiar homecoming sound of crunching underfoot. Now I'm visually confirming it. No shells at all are present here, halfway up the third set of steps.

I kill the flashlight and darkness, complete and total, hustles in to surround me.

Okay. I kneel, wincing, and feel for the latches on the briefcase. The lock is already spun into its correct open position. Six-six-six. Locating the latches, I ease the case open.

I'm not 100 percent familiar with this particular handgun, but I've seen it assembled and so I go through it slow, massaging each component and sliding it into place as quietly as possible.

Sig Sauers are pretty intuitive and user-friendly.

A couple things occur to me now. One: whoever is here is probably already aware that I'm here as well. And two: the suitcase came with some nifty night-vision goggles.

I slide my hand around until I hit them, feel for the front of the gadget, remove my hat, and pull them over my head and into place. That's better. I replace my hat.

Blood tint my world.

And I almost puke from the force of what is unmistakably a "memory": moonscape-like vista, made unreal by the red tinge that brought on this vision, I see a tank, a Humvee, two or three civilian vehicles, a cart and some livestock, visible heat waves shifting near the ground, and a couple low houses. In the middle distance, a hitherto unseen man casually stands up, starts making hand signals to unseen persons or person behind him. I squeeze off a shot, his chest explodes, and I understand that a short-term goal has been accomplished.

Wham. I'm back in the present but Jesus that shakes me up. My perspective had been through some sort of infrared scope.

What did I do that would cause my brain to be so completely fragmented regarding certain things, and so photographically specific in its recall of others?

What did I do?

Can't go there now. Won't go there. I hear my mother's voice: *If not now, when?* To which I say, *If I had my way, never*.

I close the briefcase, remove my shoes and socks, and leave them on the staircase. Proceeding then down the hallway leading to the Reading Room, holding my gun and flashlight crisscrossed in the manner of all law enforcement, at least as depicted by Hollywood. Why? Habit. Plus it looks cool.

I note: the generator has been turned off. Godamnit, how did they find the fucker? Further, there has been extensive tampering, as the battery-powered camping lanterns I had hung down the length of the hallway are not illuminated. Pain in my ass. If this turns out to be some kids fucking around . . .

Pausing near the entrance to the Reading Room

(because it would naturally be here that anyone would come; the Reading Room is the heart of this place and it has a special magnetism), I listen closely to determine if anyone is just inside the doors. Ninety seconds and I'm satisfied that if I have guests they're further within the huge space.

I crouch and slowly rotate my body into the hall. I'm very pleased to notice that the goggles are heat sensitive, so hot dog! Right away I spy two individuals, one wedged between wall cases on the west side of the room, one on the east—I can see him only partially as the benches block my view.

Note another man stand up and move slowly west across the room to join his companion.

Three men total. I think. Touch my key for luck.

Sizing this up, it appears to me that the fellow on the easternmost side was in the middle of going through my belongings when my presence was detected. I can see that my gear is not properly placed in my preferred nook, which is just to his right.

Based on this, I'm assuming that this man will be the most dangerous, and the most useful of the three in terms of answering questions I might have; and that the other two are most likely along for added weight.

I wish I could see more of the man to the east; I want to disable him, but all I've got is a partial view of his head and chest. That won't do.

Decisions are made for me, which is just as well, as one of the two fellows to the west begins to move quickly in my direction, feeling his way along the wall so as not to trip on the long tables. I doubt if I've been spotted, I reckon he's been told to go cover the door.

The trouble with the night-vision goggles is that anything warm-blooded appears to be nothing but a glowing shape, like that smudgy picture of the hoax Yeti. I don't get a lot of detail, especially when they're in motion.

At any rate, I go ahead and draw a careful bead on the moving figure, and shoot him in what I hope to be the head. I seem to have hit him as his lungs evacuate and he disappears behind the tables.

The other two are in motion now, and of course they saw the muzzle flash so I'm moving too, in an easy sideways roll. Foremost I want to disable the man who was digging through my shit, and he's up and running toward my previous position.

I take a calculated gamble, keeping half an eye on the other guy, and I wait till my first target has emerged from behind the row of tables. As he does so, I fire from about fifteen feet out at what I hope to be his leg, trusting I don't hit an artery, this in tribute to Iveta Shapsko, as that was such a simple gesture and one almost forgets to opt for nonfatal options in emotionally charged situations like this.

But me, I'm at a remove from the emotional world. I feel disembodied, analytical, and it's a very pleasant sensation. Feels like a safe place.

Man number one, as I think of him, goes crashing face forward, bouncing off the edge of a table, and begins shrieking like a banshee. Which jars me out of the zone, it seems so totally inappropriate, this being a library and all. I wanna shush him just on principle, start thinking sloppy. Therefore, I momentarily lose connection with man number three, who I can no longer see.

There's a break in the action, an intermission.

Number one is now on the ground, he ceases screaming, jagged breathing for a moment . . . Suddenly he's speaking, it's Slavic . . . it's Serbian, and my Serbian is a little rusty . . . He's calling to God or his buddy, calling out my position perhaps.

So I roll gently out into the middle of the aisle that separates the two table banks and bisects the room, reckoning, correctly, that man number three is moving cautiously down said aisle, approximately twenty feet away.

I take about three seconds to make sure I get in a chest shot, which I follow up as fast as I can with a bullet to the skull. The guy drops to his knees, remains there for a moment, and falls sideways, most likely dead before he connects with the floor.

Man number one has been speaking all the while; as I listen I can feel my brain adjust and the language becomes more and more comprehensible. He's saying, "Shoot two meters to the left of my voice, shoot low." As I'm processing this he gets off a bullet that grazes my ear, incredible if indeed the guy isn't able to see in this darkness. All sound on that side is converted to a high-pitched tone, and I feel warmth . . .

I'm concerned about my suit so I fall sideways, quick, catching myself and sliding to the left, ensuring (hopefully) that I can keep blood off my collar and shoulder. I've got a great view of man number one now, who is frantically trying to determine if he hit me or not, waving his pistol this way and that.

I can take my time to steady myself and have a long look at my target. Once I'm satisfied with this, I shoot him in the hand, which causes him to lose hold of his gun, which lands between us.

From there it's a simple matter of sliding over to him, laying down my pistol for a moment, and grabbing his weapon. I jam it down the back of my pants and pick up my gun again.

He switches to English. "Hey," he says. "Hey. Okay. Enough. Hey—"

I direct the flashlight at his face and turn it on, still lying sideways. This is a white man, mid to late thirties, slightly overweight, a large scar creating a second mouth below the one he was born with, crew cut, polo shirt, and jeans. His eyes are rolling backward as if trying to get a look at the top of his head. I slide still further in his direction.

The man seems to be going into shock, so I backhand him with the flashlight. He sputters and his eyes double back toward me, though he doesn't look particularly frightened, just confused . . . He's got a hole in his thigh, thankfully the blood that continues to collect is just shy of my elbow.

Anyway, I think I have his attention. "Give me your shirt," I say in Serbian.

"Hey," he says in English to the ceiling. Then, in Serbian: "What?"

"I said give me your goddamn shirt, and don't bleed on it."

It appears painful, I get a look at his hand, destroyed as it is by my last shot, his pinky gone, ring finger missing above the second joint. Damn, I didn't intend to do that much damage. He manages, heroically, to work his shirt off with getting too much blood on it.

I snatch it, ball it up in my left hand, and press hard on my ear. Then I stand up. Stomp on his kidney once, twice for good measure. Bare feet, but still. If this suit is ruined, so help me . . .

Pull the jacket off, awkwardly trying to hold his shirt to my ear as I do, and throw it over a bench. It looks okay but it's impossible to tell through the goggles. Did I mention this was my last good suit?

This guy isn't doing much more than groaning, and won't be going anywhere soon. It'd be best if he didn't bleed to death, as he and I need to have a talk, so I hobble over to his buddy, another husky fellow plus a beard.

It was a clean head shot with a perfectly round, smallish entry wound, messy in the back where the bullet left his skull. Plus that chest shot . . . I got to say it: I'm pretty tight when it comes to the gunplay. Just saying. I don't examine him, rather I tear off his T-shirt, rip it into two pieces.

I go check on the other guy across the room real quick. Yup, I hit him dead on, through the right eye socket. He's still moving around, so I kneel and place my gun under his jaw, his left eye radiating panic, and fire, the bullet passing though the top of his head.

This done, I return to man number one. Say, "Your people are dead. But for you, sir, I'm going to wrap up these wounds, show you I'm a . . ." I search for the correct Serbian idiom. "A reasonable kind of guy."

I pull on a pair of surgical gloves that I'd kept in my back pocket. Switch back to English.

"So, my man. Kindly don't do anything stupid . . ." Which is overkill because this fellow isn't capable of much at this point.

I create a tight tourniquet above his leg wound, tie it off. Wrap up his wrecked hand, loosely. I feel a tad bit bad about the hand, that's not going to ever be remotely the same should he live through this. Which, alas, I couldn't allow anyway. Ah well.

Word to the motherfucking wise: don't be a punk-ass creep who prowls around other people's homes, goes through their stuff, then waits for them in the dark. People might rightly assume you mean them harm and react as they see fit.

Squatting next to the guy, I put the flashlight in his face. His eyes dilate, which I take as a positive.

"Hey. Sunshine. I don't dig getting shot at. Especially by a bunch of unattractive dudes." The man's breathing is labored, noisy. He may be going into shock, so I speed it up. "And I don't dig it when people go through my stuff. What do I call you?"

For the time being, I lay the three bodies out on the roof, feet-toward-park so they don't roll down the slight incline. Morning showed up an hour ago, shaping up to be one of those opaque cloud-covered migraine-type days that slow cook you like a boiled egg.

I'm just too freaking tired to do anything else with these folks, and I have yet to deal with my ear, beyond duct-taping a ball of polo shirt to my head. I am stripped to the waist, and I chew off a chunk of yak jerky, which is the consistency of tar but does the job of keeping me standing.

The Empire State Building is looking majestic as ever—despite the 2/14 massacre on the observation deck, it appears exactly the same as it did prior. Why shouldn't it? Likewise the Chrysler Building. What happened there? I don't remember.

From this vantage, I'll be able to toss the corpses into the garbage pits in Bryant Park, whereupon they will be burned, hopefully unnoticed. It seemed like a good plan earlier, but by the time I dragged the third man up here I was close to passing out from the exertion. Maybe I've lost blood as well.

Thankfully for those of us who need to wrap up dead bodies and suchlike, painters had been working on the main hall at the time of the building's evacuation, so there's plenty of burlap tarps with which to swaddle bodies, like babies, should the need arise.

I leave them there, three bundles of joy.

Anyhoo, I didn't get much out of the main man. But what little I did get seems pretty promising: his name, his ID, and a photograph.

I shuffle down the stairwell, and as I reach my floor, I pull the smudged scrap of paper out of my back pocket. As he was dying, I asked if I could do anything for him. The man said yes, tell his family he's sorry. Hence the occasion to obtain a written name. I never got to ask where his family is, not that I have time for tangents like that.

The ID card has him down as *Goran Milankovich*, in the employ of Do Rite Construction, with an address on Little West 12th. Likewise, his two buddies carry cards reflecting the same employer.

I peer at the scrap again. The lettering in Goran's hand is a form of Cyrillic that I assume is Serbian, but apparently my reading comprehension isn't up to the same level as my command of the spoken language. This happens sometimes.

The biggest surprise, however, is the photo. It's a crappy print on regular paper, but it's clearly Iveta Shapsko. She's quite a bit younger, and is smiling for the camera. She wears a sundress or a strappy loose top (it's torso up), and a body of water is visible behind her. There's a low wall as well, painted blue and white, vibing Mediterranean. On the flip side are more of these Cyrillic scribbles. I get goose bumps as I clock the English characters, *42nd/5th Ave.*

My address. On the back of a photo of Iveta.

So, despite my exhaustion, the last thing I do before giving my ear some attention is to pull out the *Library of Congress Russian Transliteration Table* and check this text against the chart of all known Cyrillic alphabets. Just to be positive. In about five minutes I'm sure the writing is of Serbian origin, describing the library's entrances.

What's with all the Serbs all of a sudden?

Close the book, thinking goddamnit. Yakiv spoke of a Serbian man, the father of Iveta's kids. Was it Branko Jokanovic? I think I have that correct. A "war criminal," no less. Sounds like a joke, dubious at best. But no more so than any other detail of this assignment, about which I've gotten lots of information but essentially know nothing. I don't even know what the assignment is anymore.

As I lope toward the bathroom (the water is still running somehow, tainted, it's a sort of amber; hell no, I wouldn't even allow it to touch my clothes), I wonder why these Eastern European people can't keep their local drama confined to the fucked-up region from whence they came. Always some kind of static or shadiness going down in their circles, it always boils over, poisoning other citizens' business . . .

Stop. I need to check this mind-set. I realize that it's exactly this kind of xenophobic thinking that was exhibited by villains like J. Edgar Hoover, certain members of the LAPD in the mid-twentieth century, Bush II, the KKK. Slippery slope.

I peel off the latex gloves and drop them in the trash. Tap my key. Assess my ear. Call it barely grazed. Little tiny bit of cartilage is missing, that's it. Lucky stuff. Not much blood either.

Applying some rubbing alcohol I consider whether it's wise to stay here and sleep. The answer to that is of course not. I douse some paper towels in the alcohol, take down my pants, and scrub my entire body. It hurts but it makes me want to sleep less.

Viewing myself in the mirror, it's a fact that I look like a bit of an undead train wreck. Ribs protrude, I can see the top of my pelvis. My neck looks like a suede rope. I need to be taking better care of myself, finding more consistent food sources.

Meanwhile, I have to figure out what the fuck to do.

The System has a basic tenet, which is really just the same kind of logic they beat into us in the military. When you're lost, make an inventory of what you know.

Item one: the district attorney has hired me to kill Yakiv Shapsko, which he assumes will occur today. He is monitoring me electronically.

Item two: Yakiv Shapsko has hired me to kill his wife Iveta. If I fail to do this he will kill me. Likewise, Shapsko is monitoring me electronically.

Item three: some Serbian entity, who may or may not be Iveta Shapsko's ex-flame/captor Branko Jokanovic, is looking for Iveta and myself, and has somehow connected her to either me or this address or both.

Item four: Iveta Shapsko's location is not known.

Pulling my pants back on, I wonder where my shoes are and remember setting them down in the stairwell. With the briefcase.

In about three minutes I'm dressed again, and I've swapped out shirts. I had blood on my collar, maybe it's salvageable but it won't do to walk around looking all nasty.

I crack open the manila folder Yakiv gave me.

Iveta Shapsko (née Balodis), aged thirty-nine, Latvian national, height five foot six inches, weight 127 pounds, brown hair, green eyes . . . Hold on.

My gear is strewn everywhere but I locate the file the DA gave me. Plop it next to Yakiv's. They're identical, down to the photo of her in the aisle of a grocery store. It's the same information, the same font, the same format. Must have come from the same source. Identical.

Not totally identical. In addition to the location in Queens, I see Yakiv's file on Iveta contains an additional address.

Okay, that's odd.

It's an eyesore of a high-rise at Columbus Circle: 1 Central Park West, the Trump Tower. I can't come up with a connection there.

Time to get organized. I locate my shoulder holster, within which I house both my Beretta and the new Sig Sauer. The Serb's gun is one of those CZ-99s. I've heard good things about them but I appreciate how that Sig performed, and of course my Beretta is like family. I stash the CZ-99 with the rest of my shit.

As an afterthought I get out my Kevlar vest, despite the heat outside, which only serves to make me look like I have a normal-sized torso.

Otherwise: I repack the briefcase with a six-pack of Purell™, a green box cutter, extra surgical gloves, plenty of ammo, the goggles, flashlight, camera, my files, toothbrush, a ziplock bag of pistachios, jerky, and two pairs of underwear and socks. Confirm I have the key, front pants pocket. Both of Iveta's files in hand.

I repack my kit bag and place it back in its nook.

It's 7:45 a.m. Don't know what I'm going to do when that wall clock, which is probably as old as the building, dies. And I still don't know my next move. Fuck it; if I sit still I'm gonna sleep, and if I sleep I'll likely get myself dead.

Press my hat back on, wince as it touches my bad ear, pop a pill, and point myself at the rear exit.

Outside, that smell. The Big Stench.

As I pass the burning garbage pits, I chuck Iveta's files into the flames.

Left, left, and left again, letting the System be my guide. I flop westward almost as far as one can go, and hang yet another left. To breathe is akin to inhaling a hot liquid plastic. If I wasn't used to it, I'd fucking choke.

Pickup truck rattles past, the open bed full of Chinese men supporting a slab of marble between them. A couple give me hard looks. Fuck those dudes. At least they know what they have to get done today, however menial. I'm still trying to get my schedule straight and nobody's going to be giving me a helping hand.

Regardless, I'm heading down Eleventh Avenue. Smelling the Stench, smelling the contaminated water.

Working on a plan.

I got to figure the DA expects to see me drop in on Yakiv, so one future stop on the gimp train is Odessa Expedited, which by chance I will nearly walk past on my way further downtown.

Cause first: let's have a look at Do Rite on Little West 12th and see what gives.

Past the car dealerships, where fossil fuel–only Lamborghinis and Bentleys collect dust. Past the husks of fancy restaurants and hot spots gone cold and empty. I pass the bones of Mario Batali's last and least successful eatery.

Brings to mind the Midtown Militia. In my opinion, they're most likely one of these urban myths, like the

Central Park Sasquatch. Keep people scared. Control mechanism. But if these tales are to be believed, you've got a roving pack of former hedge-fund managers, Wall Street types, armed to the gills with carbines and shotguns, who will open up on anything resembling an official vehicle or individual. The story goes, these men and women saw the writing on the wall precrash, and converted their collective wealth into gold bars. Which they hold in storage in an underground vault, somewhere near the former UN building. Hoping to wait it out.

You hear stories, stories about intrepid treasure hunters who set out, like Cortés, seeking the fabled City of Gold. And you hear stories of these brave souls washing up on Brighton Beach, their bloated, waterlogged bodies riddled to mesh by .45 caliber holes.

And of a patrol, usually on Madison Avenue, stumbling upon a set of decapitated heads, mounted on the poles that formerly demarcated bus stops for the notoriously slow M1, 2, or 3 uptown local routes.

Who can say? Anyway, I've got plenty more to worry about at the moment.

Here we are. Hang a left on to Little West 12th Street. It's early yet, but there's no activity whatsoever, which is surprising. A forklift in the middle of the street.

I past the old Standard Hotel, which shows signs of inhabitation. Trust it: the designer hotels will be the last to go, cause the folks with the money need somewhere to lay their crowns.

The address I have is 14 Little West 12th, and I come upon the spot, the street number spray-painted in yellow across the metal pull-down shutter. Closed up tight. Is it a Sunday? Does anyone still pay attention to that stuff?

To the left of the garage-style entrance is a glass door with the number 14 on it. There's a buzzer marked *Do Rite*, among others. I try the door, locked. Press random buzzers, avoiding the one for Do Rite.

Nobody home. After waiting a spell, what the hell, I take out the Beretta and smash a hole in the glass. Remove my jacket, wrap it around my hand, reach in, and after some groping I open the door from the inside. Straightforward stuff.

I mount the stairs, putting my jacket back on, grimacing at my goddamn leg . . . On the second landing, down a narrow hallway, I locate a door with a plaque announcing *Do Rite*. The building is dead quiet and dark. I take this opportunity to take a pill. Note: I have three pills left.

What the hell, I pull on surgical gloves and knock three times, hard. Wait, with my ear to the door, holding the Beretta loosely.

Pretty sure nobody's around. I back up and brace myself against the wall. The door splinters on my fourth kick; the knob falls off and rolls down the hall.

Not very subtle, but I never did learn to pick a lock.

Dark in there. I open my case, get the flashlight, turn it on. Feel my key nervously. Proceed inside.

Threadbare wall-to-wall carpet, smelling of mold. Office Depot file boxes stacked up, flanking the hallway. The boxes are dated, I run the light over them for a good while. Seemingly they run from 2003 to present. I move on.

A larger room, a couple cubicles with manual typewriters and cheap chairs. On the walls, an idyllic looking beach scene, with *Cyprus* in a flowery script. A muscle-cars calendar, with a photograph of a Dodge Charger, open to the correct month and year. Also, a map of the lower half of the city, with four white thumbtacks, all marking points in the financial district.

Another door leads me into an office, sunlight entering through diminutive windows. I switch off the flashlight and scan the room.

Rather orderly, lots of papers in English and two different types of Cyrillic—one I recognize as Russian, the other is the Serbian variant. A small workspace with a desktop PC and what looks like an Orthodox icon.

I take a second to flip through the nearest stack of papers . . . invoices, etc., correspondence, all legit business stuff, pretty dry, in English, Russian, and Serbian, all of which are signed by one Brian Petrovic.

I scratch at my new microchip, thinking.

Then my eye is drawn to the middle of the room. A coffee table, upon which stands an intricate scale model of what is unmistakably the Freedom Tower. I look at the model for a second, trying to figure out what's wrong.

Then I see it: there's an extra tower, made for some reason out of what looks like rosewood. I nudge it lightly and it wobbles. It's loose, not part of the mock-up at all.

I pick up the box carefully. It's about three inches wide and five inches tall. Smells like rosewood. I give it a gentle shake, something shifts. Turn it over a couple times. It's featureless, save an engraved symbol that even I recognize as a Byzantine-looking cross, with that small extra crossbar running diagonally near the base. Could be Greek Orthodox. Could be Serbian Orthodox too. I can't help it, all this arcane crap rattling around in my head. I like to read.

It's not immediately obvious how you open it, but after futzing with it for ten seconds it becomes clear that one side is actually a slat. It slides open down the length of the box, and I'm looking at something behind a thick plastic window. Again I'm slow on the uptake.

A couple seconds later I realize I'm looking at a mummified hand, on a patch of red velvet. A very, very old mummified hand, the color and texture of a dried apricot.

I want to assume it's simian, but examining the fingernails . . . a gibbon? Nope. I'm no archeologist, but I'm gonna say it's a human hand.

An Orthodox cross, a human hand . . .

At this very moment, I hear muffled voices. Sounds like two or more individuals, coming from the hall entrance. One of the two gives a "shh" and they go silent.

Shit. I open my briefcase and place the wood box inside. No idea why exactly, but anytime you find a human body part anywhere, it's worth paying special attention to. Just speaking from experience.

Actually, I think this particular body part is a unique item that might come in . . . handy?

Ouch, sorry.

Carefully now, I walk over and ease the door to the office shut, turn the lock. I take up a position to the left and cock the Beretta. Put my good ear to the piece of plywood that serves as the office's wall.

I'm there about three minutes when the doorknob is quietly turned, found to be locked, and jiggled quietly. On the other side of the wall I hear mumbling. Nothing happens for a few moments.

Then I see the plastic of an ID laminate slide through

the crack between door and wall, just above the knob. I realize what they're doing and tense up for it. The plastic comes down slowly and pops the lock.

As soon as I see male hands pushing the door open, I bring my gun butt down hard on the forearm. There's a yelp of anguish, he tries to bring a Glock up with the other hand, I crack him on the knuckles, the gun falls to the carpet. I then get a hold of his arm, pull him toward me, twisting his hand up and behind his back. I turn him around, jerk him close, and stick my gun in his ear. All this and I've still got a two-fingered grip on the briefcase.

I'm now facing the barrel of a pistol too, behind that a woman, maybe early thirties, brunette, dressed in a no-nonsense blue business suit. She's got some subcontinental Asia in there somewhere, her skin has a nice tawny sheen.

The man in my arms is wearing a cheap blue two-piece suit. Their attire screams "government" to me, but we'll see.

"Drop your weapon," she says, sounding a little shaky. "Drop your weapon or I'll be forced to shoot. We're federal agents."

I smile—yes sir, it's amateur hour.

"I'm happy to drop my weapon, if you'd care to drop yours first. As you can see, I've got your man here and I'm not yet emotionally attached to him."

She's blinking and her hands begin to shake a bit.

The dude wants to be hero, says: "Anne, don't you dare stand down. Take the shot. You can do it." Too many Bruckheimer movies. He's a small guy, he should take it easy.

Anne is trying to rally. "I said drop your weapon."

"Anne," I reply, "you know that if you attempt to shoot me, you'll hit us both. Okay? So why don't we all just relax, just walk it back, swap stories, and see if we can't work this out."

"Take the shot," repeats the hero.

"Look now." I stay focused on Anne. "We're all a little worked up. These are crazy times. How about we both put down our guns and just have a talk. I bet you we can all be friends. I bet we're all in the same gang. We can look back on this and laugh. Let's put down the guns."

Anne is wavering.

"Don't do it, Anne, take the shot."

"Man, do you have some kind of death wish? What is your problem?"

"Go fuck yourself."

I sigh. "Honestly, Anne, the chances of this ending badly are very, very high, unless we put down our guns. I even volunteer to go first. Okay? Here I go."

Twisting the guy's arm even further—he grunts but isn't going to give me the satisfaction of a more amplified display of pain—I force him to crouch down with me. I place the gun on the carpet. We come back to a standing position together; I feel like we're in some kind of modern dance class.

"See? Your turn."

Anne directs her gun at my head with renewed vigor and I see her trigger finger spasm. So I push her companion at her with all the strength I can generate. They collide, and are knocked to the ground. Her gun goes off, *boom!* Somebody hits their head on the flimsy partition that separates the cubicles, and that comes down as well, kicking up lots of paper.

I pull out the Sig Sauer and train it on them. They're unhurt as far I can tell, and the guy, who has Japanese features, is looking both embarrassed and furious. He's checking himself.

"Jesus, did I get hit? Am I hit?"

Anne seems stunned.

"Everybody okay?" I say.

"We're federal agents," says the Japanese-looking guy, flushed, in total disbelief, I imagine, at how wrong this scene has gone for them. "You're in enough trouble already."

"Uh-huh. Let me see your IDs."

"We're not giving you anything. Drop the gun," snaps the guy.

I'm getting annoyed. "Friend," I say, "you aren't in a particularly good position to tell me what or what not to do. Plus I don't like your tone. So just do like I say and let's see some IDs."

Anne, who is still holding her gun but seems to have forgotten about it, tosses me her laminate. Her nose is bleeding.

"Goddamnit, Anne. What are you doing?"

"I'm taking initiative, so just shut it, Mike," she says. He shuts it.

The laminate reads: *Annette Jaspreet, FBI.*

"FBI? Really?"

"Yeah. Federal agents, like we said," Anne responds. She's pulling herself together. "We're going to stand up now, okay?"

"By all means, just do it slowly."

They get up off the floor, carefully. Mike is nursing his arm. I toss them my ID. The guy scrambles for it, scrutinizes it.

"Dewey Decimal? Is that a joke?"

I shake my head.

"And you work for the city. Which means we outrank you here."

"Sure," I say, smiling, "that's fine. I don't have an ego about it. Are you going to bust me for B&E, Mike and Anne of the FBI?"

"Explain your presence in this office," says Mike.

"Okay. I was assaulted last night by three men, all of whom seem to have been employed by this company. I came down here to determine its relevance to my current assignment."

"Which is?" Anne takes my ID, studies it.

"Classified. A city matter." I smile at the two of them.

"Classified? The fuck? Can he do that?" Mike looks to Anne. "I don't think he can do that."

"Just a minute," Anne says irritably. She's keying my info into a palm-type device.

We wait. Touch the key. Tap the briefcase, the rosewood box within. A human hand, an Orthodox cross. I can feel my synapses firing, making connections I can't yet articulate.

Mike fumes. "You can't do that. We're FBI, we're not freakin townies. Local stuff can't possibly be kept classified from the Bureau . . ."

I shrug. Anne shows the handheld to Mike.

"It just says *transmitting*."

"That means it's uploading the information, it's slow, Jesus, give it a minute." She dabs the sleeve of her white blouse against her nose, peers at the blood. "Oh, okay, here it is." She's reading something. Then she tosses back my ID.

"All right, Mr. Decimal. Friends in high places. You have the get-out-of-jail-free card. Congratulations."

I hand Anne her ID.

"Thanks."

Mike is dumbfounded. "This man accosted me."

"I apologize for that, my mellow. I really do. I assumed you were from the same crew I dealt with last night."

Anne is considering something. "Look, do you mind if ask you a few questions? Just informally?"

"Why are you deferring to this guy?" says Mike, and Anne silences him with a look.

I clear my throat. "I'm not compelled to answer your questions. But perhaps we can help each other out on a couple fronts. Are you open to that?"

The two exchange glances.

Hoofing it across town, making all the necessary pre–eleven a.m. lefts.

The two feds admitted they were both kind of new. This I could have told them. The FBI being extremely shorthanded and operating, this year, without a budget, there are a lot of fresh faces.

They made me "promise" I wasn't an assassin or anything like that. Gosh golly wow! I assured the kids I was certainly nothing of the kind. They seemed satisfied with that. Mouseketeer time. Amazing.

Regardless: they didn't seem overly pleased with their current assignment, for many reasons.

I finally dragged it all out of them. "You don't have to actually say it. Just say nothing if I've got it right." That kind of psychology.

The job had been handed down from Interpol. In essence, seeking two war criminals. Thus far, the Bureau has succeeded only in getting a line on one of the two, that they are aware of. Through "local sources" suspicion was thrown here. So the scouts set out to observe the contracting firm Do Rite, and in particular determine if its owner, one Brian Petrovic, is in fact Serbian war criminal Branko Jokanovic. If so, they are to take him into custody and prepare him for extradition to the international court in The Hague, Netherlands. Ditto number two, should they ever get a line on said person.

All this, they were just jawing, telling me this stuff right there on the street. Flushed and excited about all the cloak-and-dagger, secret-agent shit.

Fuck's sake, I could be anybody. Really, is this our best and brightest? If so, my friends, we might as well just stick a fork in it, cause we're pretty well done. I should be working for the Chinese. Something to chew on.

Wondering if there isn't another reason they'd be so quick to feed me this information.

I'm moving. If my memory serves, I'm headed to West 26th Street, just off of Sixth Avenue. The sky is bruise colored, clouds herding together, making the heat no less oppressive. I hobble forth, fingering the key in my pocket.

Brian Petrovic, a Serbian national (according to his papers, which had been determined by FBI experts to be of "dubious origin"), aged fifty-eight, who immigrated in 1995 (though all these facts are in dispute), lived with a relative in the Philadelphia area until 2002, at which point he moved to New York and incorporated Do Rite. The firm's projects had at first been restricted to the Williamsburg/Greenpoint areas of Brooklyn, as the housing boom out there went into overdrive. Later, Do Rite was involved with the construction of the New Museum for Contemporary Art in Manhattan, as well as numerous residential high-rises. Currently, their biggest job is the Freedom Tower, at which they deal primarily with issues of insulation and construction of the necessary metal studs.

My FBI friends had numerous issues with their job, as mentioned, the first of which being that the subject is so goddamn boring. They have a running wiretap in his office, yielding nothing so far. They tossed his home and workplace twice, finding little of interest. A Bureau linguist is in the process of translating all of the man's work-related and personal documents, and after two months has come up with nothing to indicate he isn't exactly who he claims to be.

His movements are maddeningly predictable. They would not give me a specific address, but said he only ever moves between his home in Greenpoint to the office, then back again. Exceptions to this being his unflagging attendance of church services. Again, they would not tell me where. Clever clever.

But that's everything I needed to hear.

Gave the two all of my information, such as it was, and the DA's number. They seemed a spouting fount of intel, would have been a shame to not mine them for all they were worth.

I then split quick. But not too quick. Didn't want to look like I had a destination in mind.

Got no idea as to the schedule at the Cathedral of Saint Sava, or if it's still in operation at all, but I'm pretty damn sure it's the only Serbian Orthodox facility in New York City. This being a Sunday, I reckon they'll be open for business.

I check the clock on the old Con Edison building, which is still going strong, good old American engineering: coming up on ten a.m.

Saint Sava is very impressive, a proper cathedral in the English Gothic style, out of context in a rather industrial/commercial neighborhood. I know little of its history, except that it was initially an Episcopalian church and designed by the guy who built the Trinity Church downtown.

I guess that's more than most New Yorkers would know. Like I said, I read a lot.

Up the stairs, the heavy doors are braced open slightly. I nudge them back, register that a service is in progress, and slip inside.

A gorgeous place, really. Even for a heathen like me. I feel that calm, that sense of space. I slide into the furthest pew back. Yeah, it's a beautiful room. A series of teardrop-shaped stained-glass windows make up a sunflower-like form high above the altar. Guy in black is droning on. I smell frankincense. Almost masks the all-pervasive plastic odor. Almost.

Now where the fuck do you get frankincense in this town? Guess there's a black market for everything.

There's maybe ten people scattered about the place. That strikes me as pretty strong attendance, given the population. I have no way of knowing if "Brian Petrovic" is present, but I can eliminate the old ladies, of which there are four.

Here. I zoom in on a pair of neckless dudes—black suits, hair closely cropped . . . A row in front of them I notice the back of another man's head, similar haircut, slouching forward now as everybody moves to a kneel. I do likewise, keeping my eye on the guy, ignoring the twinge in my knee.

He looks pretty engaged. There's some chanty stuff which I don't follow, a call-and-response deal.

People sit down again. Can't get a good look at the guy. One of the neckless fellows seems antsy. He's glancing around the place, leans over and says something to the other, who elbows him. Yeah: pretty sure those are the muscle. Which makes the guy in front of them a very likely candidate.

I take this opportunity to check for my key and pop a pill; note that it's my second-to-last. Gotta get this whole scene sorted out quick, run kill Yakiv, and head back to the DA for a refill. Can't forget. Scrub up with some Purell™. I don't like having to sit on public seating, especially if it's wood. Absorbs the bacteria.

Yakity-yak, the man in black. Is Serbia even a place anymore? I'm fading, drifting off . . . jerk myself back to the moment. Think I fell asleep. I have to stay present.

Soon enough the preacher seems to be wrapping it up. We do some sort of group prayer, heads up, heads down, and then it's over. The priest disappears and folks are getting up to leave.

I stay seated, with my head slightly bowed like I'm still super into it. A couple of impossibly old ladies move past, slow as glaciers. Wait, here comes my mark, followed closely by the two big guys.

Looks older, more frail than I'd anticipated, late fifties, gray-white hair closely cropped, wearing a banana-yellow Puma tracksuit and loafers. Glasses, behind which are sad eyes.

One of the big guys double-takes me. The fuck? But they lumber on.

I let them pass on by, count to five, then pull myself from the pew.

Outside it's begun raining. The trio has paused in the entryway and one of the heavies is fumbling with an umbrella. The older man snatches it out of his hands and pops it open.

I close the distance a bit, the old man walking ahead, the fellows a few paces behind.

Wait until I've exited the church.

At the top of the stairs, what the hell. I say: "Branko Jokanovic."

A strange thing happens. The old guy keeps walking, so I have a split second in which I assume I've been mistaken. But the heavies turn and make a lunge for me. I step back to avoid them and trip on one of the stairs, go tumbling into another older lady as she exits the church. All four of us wind up in a pile. Lady commences shrieking.

I roll sideways off the woman, and the men are at once shushing her, and assisting her to her feet like gentlemen.

I could do any number of things. The older man hasn't even turned, he's heading toward a parked Navigator. Hold up. A Navi. I must have walked right past it. Dumb-ass. Smoke-tinted windows? Check.

But now the guys have the lady standing, dusting her off, they're apologizing profusely, she gives me a hateful glance and begins to move off down the stairs. The men turn their attention back to me.

I go into a fighting position and get ready for whatever's next. The guys look like they're about to rush me, when there's a single-syllable command barked at them. My brain doesn't decode it for some reason. But they freeze.

The old man is standing with the Navigator's door open. He speaks in Serbian, quieter this time, something like, "No, no, bring him over to the car . . ." And then in English, "Not here. Come." Indicates the vehicle.

The boys grab me, an arm each, and I'm pretty much carried down the stairs. Catch a look at the plates. Uh-huh, you got it. Diplomatic.

The big boys deposit my sack of bones in the backseat. Hands grope my pockets, under my jacket, get a grip on my guns, shit, my briefcase is being pulled away, they're going to just grab it—

"Wait a moment," says the main man, in Serbian. "Let him hang on to his belongings." Big guys start to protest, to which Branko adds, "Shut up. Sometimes a subtler approach is needed. Catch more flies with honey. Gentlemen, please."

They unhand me, leave me sitting upright. I brush myself off, looking for stains. Think I'm clean.

"Slide over," says the old dude, in English.

I do and he gets in next to me, keeping his gaze straight ahead.

The big boys haul themselves in up front. There's a brief conversation, and the driver takes his hand off the ignition key.

We sit in silence for the moment, the rain knocking at the windshield. The man reaches in front of him, a gold and black tissue dispenser. He pulls out three or four Kleenex. Hands them to me. "Your ear. It is bleeding."

God do I hate to take those tissues, but I do it, and I press them to my ear. "Yeah, thanks."

"So. You're welcome," says the old man. "I do not want to get off on the wrong foot. So. You can see, I give you the courtesy of retaining to your personal items. Be aware that my men have weapons too, and would cause you very much harm should you attempt anything impolite."

I nod. "Right. I understand. Appreciate the gesture."

There's another period of silence. The man closes his eyes. Just when I'm positive he's asleep, he speaks.

"Whom were you addressing when you called this name."

"I was addressing you."

"Ah. So, so. Well, you must have me mistaken for someone else. I am Brian Petrovic."

He extends his hand. I shake it and say: "Uh-huh. In that case, it's odd, how your men responded. Don't you think?"

He puts his tongue in his cheek as if trying to dislodge some food. The guys up front are sitting stiffly, face forward.

"Can I pose a question?" Nobody responds, so I soldier on. "How long have you guys been on my tail?"

Nothing.

Brian takes a deep breath and removes his glasses. Pinches the bridge of his nose. "Still," he says, ignoring my question. "You are in error, concerning my name. So."

"All right. But you are the owner of the contracting firm Do Rite?"

"That's correct."

There's another period of quiet. Then, "Goran and the others," says the man, "I am guessing you saw them."

"Yup."

"So, so." He licks his lips. "I get an idea now of who you are, sir."

"Right. And I have a sense as to who you are, as well."

"As I just said, my name is Brian Petrovic. And you

are the Negro with the interesting name, Dewer . . ."

"Dewey. Dewey Decimal."

"Yes, I see." He looks out the window. "So. Is it offensive, this word *Negro*?"

"That depends. In general I would say more obsolete than offensive. But it usually winds up sounding offensive, yeah."

"Yes, I understand."

"That's good. Brian, why did you send armed thugs up to my house?"

"Thugs, well, I don't think—"

"Well, the fact is, I came home to three guys with guns waiting to jump me."

"Do. Not. Interrupt. Me. I was explaining," says the older man, slowly.

Another pause. I'm wondering if this guy had a stroke or something.

Again he licks his lips. "So, so. I am looking for a woman."

"Aren't we all."

"You know what I mean. This woman was in your company when she disappeared. So. I am thinking you must have some idea where she goes."

"I don't know what you're talking about."

The man looks me straight in the face. "Oh, I think you do. Hmm?"

I blank him.

"Mr. Decimal. I have treated you with dignity, let you keep your things. Can you perhaps consider to return the kindness?"

I say nothing. My briefcase is wedged between my feet.

He peers out the window again. "This is so very tiresome. I would like a coffee."

He taps the driver on the shoulder, tells him something. The power locks come down with a soft thump, and the engine starts humming.

"Hey," I say, hand on the door.

We jet away from the curb.

"Come with me to Brooklyn," says Brian. "It's the place for the best coffee."

With the bridges out save the Queensboro, you have basically one choice when it comes to getting out to Brooklyn. That's the Battery Tunnel.

I don't like the idea of an enclosed space, especially when said space is a structurally compromised underground tube, with ungodly amounts of water pressure from the East River tirelessly attempting to crush it. Don't like it at all.

As we zip down the West Side Highway, virtually free of traffic, I am treated to a nice view of the Freedom Tower construction site, where work apparently continues apace even on a Sunday, and even in the rain.

This might be a kick for some, but it's strictly tourist stuff for those of us who have grown weary with what has been nothing more than a construction site for seemingly eons. Believe it or not, there are those pilgrims who still journey down here and weep for strangers, mourn America's ravaged virginity.

What a colossal waste of time and tears.

I note with amusement that the Navigator's GPS system, in a mode that indicates places of interest apparently, demarcates this area to our left as *GRND 0*. Must be an old car.

Battery Park City flashes by, and without fair warning we're in the tunnel, yellow lights coloring us jaundiced and sickly. I grip the door handle and turn my face away from "Brian" or whoever this man is. Don't want to be perceived as a pussy. I clench my eyes tight, give my key a quick check.

Think about the System: yes, it works, it protects: odd-even motorway designations, even when I'm not in the driver's seat, a good omen. West Side Highway, a.k.a. 9A . . . and I know this death hole will deposit us onto 278, a.k.a. the Brooklyn-Queens Expressway.

Of course, upon its construction, this strip of underwater roadway was known as 478, thought to be the mouth of a new road for which its planners had big ideas, never to see fruition. I only know this because I read too much. I would think the System can overlook this bit of trivia and still consider me in compliance. I don't know why this tunnel disturbs me so completely, when I'm perfectly content to ride the subway.

It's all moot when I hear the rat-a-tat of raindrops on the windshield once more. I take a long, deep breath. Wasn't so bad. Luckily, nobody's a talker here in this car. I sneak a pill.

We take the ramp and merge onto 278 eastbound, unhindered by traffic, blast past the once-genteel neighborhoods of Carroll Gardens, Cobble Hill, and Brooklyn Heights, dipping under the Promenade, to our left and across the water are sweeping views of lower Manhattan . . . If you ignore the disemboweled bridges and absence of traffic, it could be 2011 again.

Up and around the bend, I get a really good look at the wreckage of the Brooklyn Bridge. A couple cranes stand unattended. Never seen it from this angle, only the Manhattan side; there's bits left standing, but you can see how the explosives must have been spaced in order to achieve this kind of damage. Not for the first time do I admire, just from a logistical standpoint, the exhaustive thought that went into 2/14.

Past the industrial-turned-fancy-residential area known as Dumbo, and a look at the remains of the Manhattan Bridge—again, I haven't seen things from this angle. The scope, the scale, it's pretty astounding.

Past the Navy Yard, which had been in mid-rethink, now abandoned for more immediate concerns. Northeast over Flushing Avenue, up a ways and to our left the shipwreck that is the Williamsburg Bridge, completing the trinity of dead bridges, through the once-teeming neighborhood of Williamsburg, all hipsterdom up and gone, only the Dominican workers remain and even then only sporadically. The Hasidic community still holds it down, impenetrable as ever, and not quick to walk away from their sprawling cache of real estate, however worthless it might be now.

We exit at Meeker Avenue, turning on to Humboldt, which becomes McGuinness Boulevard, proceed to Huron Street, take a left, and come to a stop at an unmarked storefront near the corner of Manhattan Avenue. Unlike the more upmarket neighborhoods in Brooklyn, the bulk of the buildings around here sport metal awnings, shingled sidings, and the occasional glimpse of vinyl. It's a nice enough area, I'm just saying it's not known for its architecture.

Haven't been out here in ages and am surprised to see babushka ladies toddling along with loaves of bread and salami poking out of their bags, generally as many people on the street as one might see in Manhattan. A few shops even look like they might be in operation. Guess the Poles work for cheap. Good for them.

I'm hustled into the storefront. Jesus, the smell out here is even worse than in central Manhattan, if that's possible. I grip my briefcase.

Dim inside and thick with cigarette smoke. Automated slot machines line the walls on both sides and ancient men and women feed them with coins. Timewarp ahoy.

Hustled toward the back, through a swinging door and into yet another era, one that I've only ever seen in films, everything sepia toned, dusty wooden floor, wainscoting, a wet bar, and striped wallpaper. In the center of the room, a round table, over which the single light source, an Arts and Crafts–style brass lamp, hangs. The table sports an outsized *MILLER TIME* ashtray. That and the television mounted in the far corner are the only nods to anything remotely contemporary.

"Sit," says the man who calls himself Brian. "Agata!" he calls.

The heavies fade into corners. I sit. Set the briefcase between my feet.

An elderly form that I can only identify as female by her dress materializes from behind the wet bar, scaring the shit out of me. The crone plops espresso cups down in front of Brian and myself, saucers with tiny spoons. She is almost completely bald and sports a huge tumor on the back of her neck.

"This neighborhood," says Brian, as if reading my mind. "So much cancer. You know why?"

I have to say I am completely enjoying this scene, it's an absolute trip. I nearly forget that this is all for real. Nearly.

"No, Brian, why so much cancer?"

He bangs his loafer on the floor. "Oil. Just below this floor. Below the street. Everywhere here. So, so. Biggest spill, until BP Gulf, in United States history."

Oh yes. That rings a bell actually . . . "Right, Standard Oil? Pre-Exxon?"

Brian shrugs. "So, this detail I don't know. I only know, a lot of sick people here."

"Benzene."

"Who?"

"Chemical compound, used as an additive in gasoline. Carcinogenic. Causes cancer."

"Are you a scientist?"

"No, I just get in a lot of reading."

Brian shakes his head and grimaces like I just told him something distasteful.

The harpy is back with a Turkish-looking coffee pot.

"Very strong, hmm, we call it domestic coffee. Very good, very strong. Extremely healthy. Vitamins." He's pouring for me, thick stuff, sure, like the Turkish variety.

Old lady slams down a bag of Domino white sugar.

"Take sugar?" Brian dips his spoon into the bag, transfers the white stuff two, three times.

"No thanks." I sip at it but it's scalding hot. I blow on the cup, set it back down.

"Okay," says Brian, stirring vigorously. "So, so. Why do you choose to protect this woman?"

"Which woman?"

"Please. So."

"Hey, why don't you all tell me? You've been following me around for who knows how long."

"Why do you try to protect her? You know what she is? Hmmm?" He takes a sip. Another grimace.

I say: "I'm not protecting anybody. Save myself."

"You would not protect her if you really knew this woman. She, she would not protect you."

"We can go in circles like this all day, I don't care."

"Okay. Well, let me tell you, we can help each other."

"No, I doubt that." I sip my coffee.

"So, so. You want work?"

"I'm fine in that area."

"Oh yes? Let me tell you. I give you the best job, you do absolutely nothing, make lots of money. Sound good?"

"Sure. Just like that, and you give me a job?"

"Yes, just like that."

"Tell me more, Brian."

"Construction site, you go in the morning, relax, have a coffee; at night, so, you go home."

"And I suppose you're hiring me on the basis of how good I am at being tailed, or maybe simply my skills vis-à-vis relaxing and having coffee? No catch? No quid pro quo?"

He grins. "Quid pro quo. Latin. Yes, there is always quid pro quo. I have already given you a service in not disarming you. A show of trust, correct? We agree?"

Shrug. "Yeah, agreed. You've shown some trust. I told you I appreciate it."

Brian nods. "So. You tell me where this woman is."

"Ah, I get it . . ." I pause, calculating this thing, continue, "Let me see, I actually might have an idea of whom you're talking about. Yeah, I think it's coming back to me."

"Please, with these games. So, so, do you want to have an arrangement or no?"

"Well it's like this, see." I slide my cup out of the way and lean forward. "I know a woman, the one I think you keep mentioning."

"Okay, now we are having a conversation."

"But I'm very sorry to say, I don't know where she is. That's the truth. In fact, I might as well be asking you, cause I'm looking for her too."

Brian considers this, staring into the middle distance. Then: "I don't believe you. So, for the last time. Where is the woman?"

"This is unfortunate, you know, because I honestly, hand to God, do not know where she is."

Brian casts his eyes left and right, says something in Serbian. I sense movement in the corners and I'm pulling both guns and standing, squeezing off two bullets apiece, *boom boom* in stereo. I've never attempted this kind of rock-star move before, but I'm feeling pretty fancy, and I've been thinking about it since we sat down.

Both big men are hit, and both big men go down hard. After this, it gets very quiet. My ears are ringing. Gotta say I'm kinda surprised that panned out.

Brian takes another sip of his coffee. Finishes it off with an "ah." Showing me he's gangster like that. "So, so," he says, "I see I have wildly miscalculated. Made a very stupid mistake, letting you keep these guns."

I nod. "Yeah, looks that way."

He tilts his head to the right. A loud crack, coming from his neck. "Foolish old man I am. Making such mistakes. It was a gesture of peace. I am . . . an optimist, this is my failing. Will undo me in the end." He coughs, eyes on me. "So. But then again, I have been told you are a psychotic."

I don't disagree. We look at each other. One of the heavies is murmuring in the corner.

"So. Please, put him down," says Brian.

"I'm sorry?"

"He may have failed me, but I don't like suffering that is not needed. This situation, I take full blame for my bad decisions. Please."

Okay.

Without taking my eyes off Brian, I walk sideways over to the big guy, glad I can't really see his eyes in this light, and I plant one in his forehead. He seizes up, and is still.

"And please, yes, the other man."

I cross the room, again keeping Brian in focus, point-blank shoot the prone heavy, dead or dying, straight in the brain-pan.

Brian has a half-smile playing across his face. "You are a born killer. So, so, I see that now. That's very sad. Mental illness, this is always sad."

I swallow. I don't like people talking smack about that which they know nothing. Making assumptions. "No sir, I defend myself when I need to. By my math, this is the second time you have directed your people to do me harm."

He shakes his head. "No, no. I have seen so many violent, heartbreaking things in this world. I see you too. Very natural." Whatever. He's on a Zen Yoda trip, says, "So, so. Maybe then this is what you've done to the three I sent to your home? Goran?"

I shrug. He nods.

Time to bow out. "Brian," I tell the man, "or whoever you are, I am now leaving and I won't be followed. Do you understand?"

"I will find you," he answers, "and when I do, I will kill you five times over, once for each man. It will be better for you, then you can rest."

This is when I play my trump card. Christ, I hope I'm right about this. "No you won't, and here's why." I holster the Beretta, keep the Sig on him. Walk back over to the table, open my briefcase one-handed. Pull out the odd wooden box, hold it up. "Recognize this?"

Brian is very still. I'm trying to read him. "No, I do not," he says, but his voice is a touch choked.

"Oh, so you don't mind if I . . ." I place my gun against the object, cock the hammer.

"Stop," he says. "So. Okay."

Ha. "The hiding-in-plain-sight thing, it's bullshit. Doesn't work. Especially when the people digging around in there don't know you're hiding anything."

Brian doesn't respond.

"It took me a bit, but if this is what I think it is? You'll take me seriously when I say that if you or your men come near me ever again, I will destroy this ugly-ass thing in a heartbeat. Trust that."

Brian remains still. He's growing ashen.

"I'm pretty sure," I say, "that your countryfolk are looking for this object. And I'm very, very sure they would not take kindly to thieves, not with something so precious as this shit."

Brian speaks: "You are the thief, Mr. Decimal."

"Well, you say tomato. I'm calling this life insurance. I don't have a fancy fucking car and a bunch of big dudes at my beck and call. Remember, you started this jive, not me."

Brian is silent.

"So now, I'm walking out this door, and if I get the slightest sense that anybody is following me, or should you attempt anything silly, this here thing gets thrown on the fire. Understand?"

Brian nods calmly. "I understand. So, so. You have my word."

I reopen my briefcase, slip the object back in, eyes and weapon trained on Brian, who looks like he's meditating. "Great. Good luck to you, Brian." I back toward the door, turn, and exit.

Walk swiftly toward the main entrance. The front room has mostly cleared out (gunshots will have that effect), the few old-timers who remain don't give me so much as a glance.

Out on the street, holy God, the air, the Stench, it's like a physical blow. Unlike the other day, if anything the rain *amplifies* its power.

I try to pull it together.

I look right and left. Start moving just to put some distance between me and the storefront. I consult my internal map, which does Brooklyn slightly worse than Manhattan. I note the G train, maybe three blocks away, dismiss it, they don't run that ridiculous route anymore.

Jesus. The G train.

Let's be real, Brooklyn and Queens: the G train was useless in the best of times.

Go to pop a pill: no dice.

Bone dry.

Oh no. Oh no. Oh Christ.

I check my pockets, turn them inside out, palm the key, pat myself down, nothing. Must've dropped them. Or did I just run out? How could I have let this happen?

Well. Contemplate the old-school slot house/coffee bar. I can't go back in there to have a look. Fucking cock-up. Have to get to the DA. Have to get to Centre Street. He'll be pissed off, but what's new there?

It's probably psychological, but the shakes set in immediately. I reckon I have about two hours before my heart explodes.

Two hours. I have to chill it out. Plenty of time. I breathe. I breathe.

I do a little Purell™, suck some more hot plastic air, push my hat down against the rain, and set off unsteadily, west. At least the general direction I need to head.

The big thing, you know, is not to panic.

I'm probably not the first to think it, but I've got to get the hell out of Brooklyn.

After John the Baptist kick de bucket at the hands of King Herod, his head was presented to Herod's daughter Salome on a silver platter, to her great delight.

Salome was one sick bitch.

But hey, most people know that much. What is lesser known is that poor John's body was then hacked into multiple pieces, and spread throughout all corners of the classical world.

The city of Istanbul claims to have John's arm, and a chunk of his skull. The Egyptians claim the very same thing. Possession of John's much-abused head is claimed by no less than five nationalities: the French, the Turks (again), the Germans, the Syrians, and the Italians. The township of Halifax in the UK even claims to have the dude's *face*, and in fact the very name of the place is derived from the Old English *halig*, meaning *holy*, and *fax*, meaning *face*.

And very much apropos the current situation: John the Baptist's right hand is said to be held by the Serbian Orthodox Church.

The hand that baptized Christ Himself.

Believe it or not, that's what I reckon I have bouncing around in my briefcase, as I stumble-swerve up Manhattan Avenue.

Apparently, Branko/Brian subscribes to this notion as well. Because I'm not being followed anymore. Am I?

I swivel and scope an old couple, white people, who recoil, even from across the damn road, and hustle off down a side street.

Look for shifty faces on foot or in cars, seeing none. I no longer think I'm being followed. Though honestly, my senses are swiftly becoming way too compromised to tell.

I taste iron in my mouth. I'm chomping on my tongue like it's yak jerky. Which in all truth tasted better than my tongue.

Making my way up Manhattan Avenue, likely the first black man ever to traverse this neighborhood in Brooklyn with the hand of John the Baptist in his pocket.

Things are all loopy, and I must get it together. Nobody's gonna do it for me.

Come on, Dewey, you just killed two hulking knots of muscle simultaneously, John Woo style. Outfoxed a for-real war criminal, if indeed that's who that cat is. Even if the idiot let me hang on to my guns, so the exit was just dumb luck.

You're a freaking badass soldier man. You can do this much.

A minivan blasts by me, I jump away from the curb. I see a beard, hat, earlocks. The van goes straight through the lights that blink yellow yellow yellow without a glance or a pause.

Tactics. Get ahead of me. Too easy. The beard, hat, earlock disguise, cheap and easy. No, no, no. I tell myself to move it. Just regular citizens doing regular citizen stuff. Jews and their minivans.

Perspective starts to shift on its axis and I stumble sideways. Straighten myself out. I take my heart rate and count to ten, System style. My pulse is through the roof. This is bad.

The rain has stopped, I barely register this and do not care. I've swung north because I want to find the Pulaski Bridge, which divides Brooklyn and Queens. Thinking I'm out of pills I'm out of pills I'm out of pills. Fuck.

I would hijack a vehicle but I'm far too shaky to drive. All I'm seeing are industrial machines anyway, forklifts.

Moving through a two-dimensional warehouse area, nothing to see even without my peripheral vision, which is fading fast, I'm out of pills, adrift in Brooklyn of all things. I'm not lost, though: I tweak left on Ash Street, I think I'm pretty close.

Limbs are stiffening up. My jaw.

I'm out of pills. A killer migraine squats behind my left eye. This is not good. I close my hand over my key, even this is not helpful. I can't connect to the System; nothing's working.

Pass a shuttered business called Pom Wonderful. What the hell could that be? Koreans, Chinese? I need to distract myself, I can't lose it out here. The wildlife will get me for sure. If my heart doesn't explode first.

Out of pills out of pills out of pills. I see the bridge. I see it. Can I get up on it from street level? I don't know.

Thank Christ, there's a metal stairwell. Can I manage it? Don't see an option. I make the stairs, slip on the wet metal, crack my shin on a stair, pull myself up, fucking drag myself up, one flight, two flights, and a third set deposits me, blinking, blind, up on the ramp to the Pulaski Bridge.

The fucking air, the ambient filth, it's killing me. I

drop my briefcase, go to pick it up, fall. Get my hand on the case and I convulse. It's really bad now. I think I start calling for help. Anybody. Come on. I can't go further. If they're tailing me I'm finished, and I don't care.

I go flat on my stomach. I think of Iveta. Thinking, I'm sorry, so sorry. I tried. Somebody with a loudspeaker trying to get my attention, but God kills the lights, and my mind just strolls away.

"I thought I might just wander around," I say to the faceless woman in the main office at Woodlawn Cemetery, "and see if I can find the, uh, site. I won't be long."

"Sir," she replies, "there are over 300,000 interment lots at this facility. It's all computerized. Might I see your lot card?"

I check my back pockets.

I check my jacket pockets.

I check my front pants pocket, feeling her eyes on me, finding only a key, feeling the panic making its way up my spine.

"Just a moment," I say to her. "I'm sure I have it here somewhere . . ."

Ammonium carbonate.

I sputter and gasp and realize my eyes are open. I'm looking at a young man in military garb, who withdraws the vial of smelling salts.

"He's up," says the soldier. "Sir!"

"Yeah, yeah, I'm okay, that's not . . ." I manage.

"Sir, are you all right?"

I lift my head. I'm halfway inside an Army Aggressor—another one? Outside is a depressing-looking stretch of elevated road. A bridge, I'm on a bridge. A couple other soldiers stand around, looking tired.

"Sir, do you have a medical condition we might need to be aware of?"

I look at the boy. Earnest and black.

He's me, before the Devil stole my soul.

"I . . . take medication."

"Sir, you lost consciousness. Do you have a specific medical condition that you can relate to me so we can better help you? What is the medication for?"

"It keeps my heart from exploding."

The kid looks at me quizzically. "Sir, are you saying you have a heart condition?"

"No, I ran out of med—"

"Washington," says another soldier from the front of the vehicle. "Wanted on the 'com."

"Sir, just relax and remain where you are. Okay?"

I nod. The soldier ducks his head and climbs into

the front of the vehicle, puts on a wireless headset. "Washington."

I glance at the roof of the truck. Metal crossbars forming . . . crosses.

"Yes sir, we have him here."

Pause. I hear a helicopter, it's far off. Or I imagine I hear a helicopter. Always, always with the helicopters.

"He mentioned medication."

Pause.

"Administer what now, sir?"

Pause. I check for my key, it's there. A constant.

"For a heart condition?"

Long pause. I fumble around . . . There's the briefcase, thank God.

"Okay . . . Right . . . I see . . . Okay . . . Yes sir . . . That's right . . . Not a problem, sir . . . Yes, just a moment." Washington climbs back to my area, says to me, "Sir, as it happens, we have some of your medication on hand, right here, so you can relax and I'll prepare that for you."

He extends the headset. I have to admit the flood of relief I feel in my stomach is enough to perk me up a bit. They've got my stuff. Everything's going to be fine. I put on the headset.

"Hello."

"Decimal, you goddamn freak," says the DA. "I hope you have. Some kinda fuckin overarching plan. That is obvious only to you. Cause you're so fuckin brilliant."

"If you'll let me explain—"

"And Decimal. What. The fuck. Are you doing. In the fuck-ass borough of Brooklyn?"

I close my eyes. "I've been asking myself that very question, sir."

There was no shucking and jiving to be done with the DA, not this time. He was buying none of it. So I came clean.

Sort of.

Now I slouch low in a car parked a few doors down from Odessa Expedited. I'm very aware of my ankle bracelet, the chip in my arm. I consider my options. All of which are pretty grim.

I was abducted, I told Rosenblatt. Shapsko's men, most likely, though I never did find out. Taken to Brooklyn. I escaped, but just barely.

Rosenblatt was not impressed.

The upshot: as far as the DA is concerned, I'm on very strict probation. Either I go to work and take care of this job, or I will be kicked to the curb. No more first-class status and, most significantly, no more medication. I will be put out in the cold. Twisting in the wind. Persona non grata. And further, I will be considered hostile to city affairs, which will be taken into consideration if I encounter any authorities.

I honestly don't know how long I could make it under such circumstances. No matter which way I approach this thing, by far the simplest solution would be to do Yakiv.

So be it.

Rosenblatt has been monitoring radio communications within Yakiv's organization, and has reason to believe Yakiv is at his office, here on West 26th Street.

This was my last chance. I would, according to the DA, find a red Volt, key, and a bottle of my medication under the driver's seat, near Odessa Expedited's address.

He stressed yet again: last chance for a slow dance. The train is leaving the station. He then gave me his private line, an honor I have not previously been granted.

Once the job is done I am to contact him, pronto, via his mobile phone. Any military personnel will be available to facilitate this with their equipment.

Committed the number to memory. Easy: 999-999-9999.

Fucking hell, man. Getting boxed in.

I pop a blue beauty and scan the buildings across from Odessa, and think I see what I want to see. The stairwell at number 247, windows facing out, across the street.

Exiting the Volt, I walk quickly to the building, try the door, which swings right open, mount the stairs, and take them up to the second landing. Simple as that.

Hungry-looking rats scatter. I crouch, which is uncomfortable but manageable. Solid view of the entrance to Odessa. With half an eye out the window, I check both weapons. This should be pretty straightforward.

I tap several times on one of the many panes in the checkerboard window, and presently it cracks. I'm able to poke my pistol through the discreet opening.

Screwing the silencer on the Sig. Might as well do the guy with the weapon he gave me. If indeed it is traceable back to Branko (Brian?), maybe we get the double bonus of painting it like some sort of funky turf thing. Who cares, really; most of all I like the idea of dropping him with the bullet intended for his wife.

I touch my ankle bracelet. Yakiv has to know I'm in the neighborhood. Like right on top of him. If I get the chance I will have to pull this off fast.

I touch my key. Nothing to do now but wait.

Don't have to wait long. Approximately twenty minutes have passed, and without preamble, a couple big guys, interchangeable with the types I've encountered in the last couple days, come out the door, followed by Yakiv himself, who is laughing with the cut-and-paste pair of thugos that take up the rear.

When he's all the way out, he pauses. I lift the gun. He's sweeping the block with his eyes, his mouth a wide grin. I have a clean shot. I start to apply pressure to the trigger finger.

Yakiv makes a rolling movement with his arms, a disco move that says, *Get on with it. Wrap it up*. I'm positive it's directed at me.

His boys hang back, exchange looks.

He's wide open, I've got him pinned, there's no way I'll miss him when I pull the trigger.

Except that I don't.

Yakiv walks into the middle of the street, looking this way and that. I withdraw the weapon. He's raking the buildings with his eyes. For a second I'm sure he's spotted me and I scoot back like a crab.

He holds his arms up, Christlike. At this point I know I'm not going to shoot the man.

Yakiv lifts his palms, shrugs, turns on his heel, and rejoins his buddies. Within ten seconds they're piling into a black Chevy van, and within another eight seconds they're gone.

I couldn't do it.

Putting aside any of the issues the DA might have with the man, his motivation to send me after him, whatever that might be, because after all I'm not particularly concerned about the finer points of city politics, putting all this aside: I don't doubt for a second that Yakiv would enjoy laying me out. Arrogant prick.

So what keeps me from carrying through? Do the job, chill out the DA. Put things right with Brian/Branko, return the hand, choke down some pills, and get back to my literary womb.

I can't do it. For fuck's sake, why?

Because this gig, it stinks. Something's not right, something's off. At the center of this tangle is an unknown quantity. The linchpin.

Iveta, around whom all this chaos orbits.

It strikes me now, this is what I've been doing all along. Chasing my own ass, trying to determine how Iveta fits in. Has she been off my mind? Not for a half minute.

I pull myself up off the floor, bounce down the stairs, and leg it toward the car, holstering my gun. Pulling out the Purell™.

That pulp cliché, the oldest of the old, the most tired of all tired phrases comes to me. But I dig the truth at its core.

When in doubt, look for the girl. Cherchez la femme.

Cherchez la femme.

There are concrete pilings, vibing Kandahar, spaced four feet apart at the mouth of the Trump International Hotel and Tower at Columbus Circle. If that isn't enough to dissuade you, there's a metal police barricade, piles of sandbags, and at least six national guardsmen sporting M4 carbines out in front too.

I steer the Volt into a spot on the park side of Central Park West and kill the engine. Wait. For a moment I forget why I'm here. Seriously. This happens, especially when I'm tired. I wonder where this fucking car came from. Stare out the front window at the dark park thinking, put it back together.

I hear a helicopter but realize pretty quick it's just in my head. Come on, Decimal, snap out of it. Look for clues. Check my pockets . . . not helpful. Notice the briefcase on the passenger's seat. Open it . . . oh yeah.

It all comes rushing back and I'm right there with it. Thank Christ I didn't freeze at a more crucial moment. It's frightening, let me tell you.

A few moments later, an overweight dark-skinned man in a gray suit pulls up in a Lexus, parking a few spaces down from me. He struggles out of the car, gives me the eye. I make like I'm concentrating on the GPS unit in the Volt, punching random buttons. He moves off, I hear the double chirp of the lock and alarm being activated.

I count to forty-five, make positive the man is headed

into the Trump. He is. Once he's through the revolving doors, I casually step out of my car. The cops aren't even remotely looking in this direction.

Understand, the smell. The Stench. Plastic, burning garbage. It's a constant. I notice it whenever I exit buildings and cars. I wonder not for the first time what exactly we're breathing.

I mosey over to the Lexus . . . Yup, there's his registration sticker right there in the windshield. *Mustafa Demir*, with a nice photo. He's allowed long-term parking radius (LPR) in this neighborhood. Means he's a resident. I think.

Too easy.

I pop the trunk on the Volt, stow my suitcase. On second thought, I open it back up and retrieve the digital camera and my bullshit Homeland Security badge. Shut the lid, make positive it's locked. Get back in the Volt. Count to sixty. Choke back a pill. Get out and head for the Tower.

As I'm approaching the entrance, the guys stiffen up, and when it's clear that I intend to go straight on in, one of them calls: "Residents and their guests only, sir."

I hail them. "Yes, I know. I'm here to visit a colleague." I hold up my ID.

"What's the name?" asks the talker of the bunch, taking a cursory glance at my ID. He's got a PDA of some kind.

"Mr. Demir. Mustafa Demir. He would have just come back from a meeting, I hope I'm not too early."

The guardsman goes to type in the name, then stops. I note his name tag says *Reynolds*, and he enjoys the rank of sergeant.

"Demir? Sure, he just walked in. Talk to the lobby staff."

I salute him, proceed.

Too easy. I take out my bogus Homeland Security/ Donny Smith badge. See, my operative axiom is this: people are kind of stupid; plus, if you've got a decent story, they want to believe you. That's because people are also lazy and don't want to have to do a bunch of extra shit.

The Trump Tower still attempts to project a rarefied aura. Lots of lights, dimmed. Must have one of those underground generators. This effort at respectability includes having a civilian staff, which is absolutely perfect for my purposes.

I approach the black kid behind the desk designated *Reception*, take him for midtwenties, well-tailored suit, solicitous smile. They make an effort here, even if this kid is the sole member of the "lobby staff."

I put the badge in his face. "Good day, sir. I need to have a word with your boss."

The kid is reading the badge, he looks ruffled for a moment but regains his cool. "That . . . that would be me, I am the day manager, sir, how can I help you?"

Another young black man, uncorrupted. I'm haunted by these kids. I lower my voice. "Son, I need your complete cooperation with regard to a national security matter."

People love this stuff. Deep down. "Ah, yes . . . yes, of course." His eyes flit behind me to the soldiers out the door. "Did you speak to—"

"Sergeant Reynolds, yes, but as our investigation encompasses guardsmen activity, I am bound to not raise this situation with one of their ranks. Understand?"

The kid is doing his best. "Yes sir."

"And I would ask you not to make any kind of signal or communicate with the men outside until our conversation is complete. Understand?"

The kid nods.

"Thank you. Son, if you'll furnish me with a list of permanent residents here, as well as guests over the last few weeks . . . Do you have some sort of visitors' log, where people sign in?"

"Uh. Yes, we do."

"I'll be needing to look at that as well. For the last several weeks, please."

The young dude looks seriously pained. "Sir, the difficulty . . . the problem is that we're not supposed to give out that information without—"

"Did I mention this is a national security issue? Son, we . . . What's your name?"

"Reginald."

"Reginald, we have reason to believe there may well be an *active* hostile cell operating in this very building in collaboration with the very military body assigned to protect it. Am I making myself clear?"

"Yes sir, very clear."

"That was more than you should know. I need you to just stay calm and give me those records as if it were the most natural thing in the world."

The kid cannot believe he got stuck with this. He is looking around for some sort of assist, but it's just not happening for him.

"I'm willing to do that, sir, but I will need to take down your badge information. And it'll take a moment for me to print out the residential list . . ."

"Fine, thank you, Reginald." I hand him my badge, which he accepts with very twitchy hands. "Take your time."

I try to angle myself so a decorative column blocks the guardsmen's view of me.

Reginald hands me a leather-bound ledger. "This dates back to the end of May. Let me just, uh, work on the printouts . . ."

"Thanks, Reginald. This is a true service to your country, you'll see."

He tries to smile but fails, then leans over a battered PC.

I flip the book open . . . As expected, it's divided into columns: visitor, who they came to see, time, etc. I know I don't have a lot of time so I just work backward from the most current entries. Flipping pages. This morning's entries, I flip past them, scanning names, times, nothing. Keep flipping. Yesterday. My eye goes past it but my stomach churns. I zoom in on : *B—l—is*, yesterday, about 8:15 p.m.

I can't read a few of the letters. My gut flips and flutters. The column for whom the guest would be going to see is blank.

Iveta Shapsko, maiden name Balodis.

I fumble in my pocket for the digital camera I pulled out of my suitcase. Futz with the lens cap, get it off. Snap a picture.

"How's that list progressing, Reginald?"

The young man looks frazzled. "It's just . . . it doesn't see the printer. Nobody uses this thing. Let me go plug it in directly." He exits, into what looks like a small office.

I flip some more pages. Day before yesterday. Looking, looking . . . yeah, there it is again. *B—l—is*, in the same hand, could be another *l* in there, or a *d*. Again, no other information save the time, 10:30 p.m. I get a picture here too.

Back to the most recent signature. Wait a second. I hold my finger in place and turn the pages to the earlier one. Yeah . . . in both instances they're in the same hand. Again, no other information . . . except the time, 8:15 p.m. and 10:30.

The kid reemerges. Goes to the computer. "Okay, this should work now . . ."

"Reginald, let me ask you something. The names in this book, this is dedicated to guests, visitors? And they're visiting residents, for the most part?"

"Yes sir, our policy is that anyone who is not a permanent resident signs the book. It's printing, I think, just a moment." He disappears again.

"Sir!" The voice of God.

I nearly drop the ledger. It's Sergeant Rock. Standing just inside the doorway. I place the register on the desk and close it casually. Reach in my pocket, brush my hand over the key for self-control.

"Are you not being helped?"

"Yes, I am, just . . . waiting." I give him a you-know-how-it-is hand gesture.

The sergeant looks around. I'm thinking, turn around fuckface and goose-step right back out that door.

But no. Of course not. He moves toward me, taking out his PDA. "You're a guest of Mustafa Demir, correct?"

"That's right. He actually told me he wasn't available for our meeting, but left some documents with the concierge for me to pick up. Regarding our business transactions."

The sergeant looks me up and down. "All right. Well."

"So the desk person is just—"

Reginald comes out of the office, saying, "Uh, sir? Here . . ." Glancing up, he freezes. Looks at me, looks at the sergeant. Looks back at me.

"Are those the documents Mr. Demir mentioned?" I ask him, my eyebrows raised, fucking roll with me, Reggie.

The kid looks back at the sergeant. The pause is much longer than I'm comfortable with. "Uh. That's right. Here we are." He offers them to me. His hands are visibly shaking.

I grab the loose pages, fold them, tuck them into my jacket's inner pocket. "Appreciated," I say breezily. Or so I hope. "Have a good evening, gentlemen." Split. Make for the door. Not too fast.

I'm out. Enjoy a lungful of heated plastic.

Phew. Fucking guardsmen. Must be really understimulated. Not even really military. I have a beef with those fucks since they smacked around my cousin out in L.A. way back in the '92 riots. Damn, that dates me, huh? Unless I'm just making all this shit up. Or it was made up for me, custom-tailored to fit.

I slide into the driver's seat with key, pulling the pages out of my jacket as I do.

Something cold and hard is suddenly pushed into my neck. Godamnit. I scope the rearview.

"Hello again, fuck-o," says Anne of the FBI.

"Agent Anne," I say, making eye contact in the mirror. "It's a distinct pleasure."

"Look." She's projecting a much deadlier aura than during our previous run-in. "I'd prefer we just make this fast and simple. No static."

"All right, let's relax. I'm always happy to be of service to the Bureau," I say.

She caught me as I was getting the papers out of my coat, my hand is still half in my jacket. I shift my reach, slow, and get a hold of the Beretta.

Anne smacks the butt of her Glock against my bad ear. I lurch to the right, hearing pink noise, and a wall of pain rushes up and tackles me.

Swearing through her teeth, she reaches around and yanks out my Beretta, throws it next to her on the backseat, then retrieves the Sig and does the same. And she hits me sideways again, on the other side of my head. I'm momentarily deaf.

She's talking, drilling her pistol into the base of my skull. ". . . fuckwad, so you need to turn down the smart-ass, turn it way, way down. Don't even speak."

Finding it hard to focus, I try nodding to indicate I understand but my muscles won't cooperate. I think she did some permanent damage. Try to tell her I missed the first part of her rap but the action is lost somewhere between synapses.

"I know your type and I have no patience for you, so

let's cut right to it."

I bring my hands up to either side of my head.

"One: you stole an item out of the Do Rite office. I want you to give it to me and I want you to do this now. And two: you know the location of a woman named Iveta Shapsko. I want that information, pronto."

My palms come away bloody. Nowhere to wipe them. I manage, "Don't have any idea what you mean, Anne, on either count."

"Okay, lean forward, hands behind your back."

I try to cooperate. Really, I do. I sense her seriousness of purpose and I'm not going to play with that. Rest my head on the steering wheel. I hear the rustle of metal on metal, and feel cuffs placed on my wrists, the ratchet of the lock engaging. She's got them on tight.

I hear her open the back door, slam it. I glance at the power lock button, make a move for it, but the cuffs prevent me. Anne pulls open the driver's-side door, grabs me by the arm.

"Out."

Bump my noggin on the roof, get to my feet unsteadily. Anne pulls the chain on the cuffs high. My sphincter spasms for a second and I let out a little hiss. She steers me around the vehicle in this excruciating yoga position, yanks the car key out of my pocket, pulls open the passenger's door, and shoves my bony self in.

Damn, this girl is strong. I misread her completely. Probably by design on her part. I blame myself 100 percent for not paying more attention. This scene is completely off the third rail and I can't find a soft spot to go for.

"I'm FBI and I'm taking this man into custody, no

need, under control . . ." Calling back to the soldiers in front of the Tower, presumably in response to a question. She's got her badge out, holding it high as she circles back around the side of the car.

Anne slides into the driver's seat. Punches me in the jaw, hard. My temple cracks against the passenger's-side window, and my hat falls off and lands at my feet.

She keys the ignition, reverses out, tires screech as she guns it up Central Park West.

My mouth is filling up with warm liquid, and I spit blood on the dash. A tooth. Try to speak. "Anne . . ."

Blowing through blinking yellow lights, accelerating . . . 63rd Street, hello, goodbye.

I slide against Anne's shoulder as she cuts a haphazard right onto the 65th Street park throughway. She breaks hard, and I'm flung forward, head-butting the windshield. The drive is cut off with police tape, piles of rock, and a fallen telephone pole.

"Shit," says Anne, then throws the car into reverse and starts backing up.

I look at the dashboard, finding blood, mucous, and the word I want to see: *Airbag*. Swinging my leg over, I bring my foot down on top of hers with all of my remaining strength, and together we press the gas pedal to the floor.

Anne screams wordlessly in my ear, tries to bite me. I bring my head up hard against her mouth and nose, hearing something crack. We careen backward across Central Park West, she's trying to pull the wheel left but loses her grip. The Volt jumps the curb and slams into a building at approximately thirty miles per hour.

There's a lull, relative quiet, joined by a new sound. Dry rubber on glass.

Think I've been blinded. I work my head to the left, see a mop of thick dark hair resting on a big gray balloon. The wipers are on.

I struggle to sit up . . . Air bags, the air bags activated. As advertised. Having borrowed that maneuver from some movie I saw on a plane ages and ages ago. Remember thinking, yeah right, no fucking way that'd work for anybody.

So I'm pretty pleased it panned out. Jah be praised.

My door has been bent and forced partially open, the entire car jackknifed. I start pushing on it with my upper arm. Apparently Anne is awake, because she grabs a handful of my hair. I shake her off and slide out the door onto the pavement, landing on my shoulder.

I think about the briefcase in the trunk.

Struggling up, I turn to see Anne has her gun out and is fighting with her door.

Fuck me, it's hard to stand up with a bad knee and no use of your arms. But I make it happen. No choice. I need to beat a retreat. I aim for the park, my hands completely numb, blood cut off by the cuffs.

Her first shot goes slightly wide, kicking up a chunk of asphalt just to the right in front of me. I don't turn around. And I doubt she'll miss twice so I just charge headlong toward the low wall next to the 65th Street transverse.

I hear the next shot as I'm flipping myself over the wall and onto a steep, muddy embankment. I slide perhaps ten feet, leaves and dirt fill my mouth, and my fall is broken abruptly as I collide with a tree trunk. I'm winded, I wheeze, sucking at the air as if through a dandelion stem.

Anne comes over the wall, skids, and collapses backward, landing on her tailbone, her skirt riding up over her midsection. She's lost a heel, kicks off the other shoe, and scoots toward me, rather gracefully, on her butt. Catches an adjacent tree, steadies herself, and trains the gun on me. Her mouth is contorted, a red messy wreck.

I spit out leaves, blood, pebbles. We're both panting. Can't seem to straighten my eyes out, pretty sure I'm concussed.

"Asshole. You broke my nose," she says, nasal.

I try to regain control of my lungs, whisper-croak: "Sorry."

"The box," says Anne, spits. "And the woman. Spill." She looks demonic; my vision is dimmed but her eyes and bloody teeth remain bright. "Woman's back at the Trump, right? And the box, it's in the car? Yeah? Am I right?"

My head lolls back, but I can speak. "Who you working for, Anne?"

She laughs. "Fuck you. Who are YOU working for, mister? Cause nobody can tell. Hey, you think anybody can get by on a government salary? I've got a six-year-old girl and student loans straight up my ass. Harvard fucking Law. Brian pays me triple. I'm still FBI but I freelance. Like you, Decimal. So fucking what."

I had started to slip away, but I drag my head back. All I can think is, I'll never get the dirt out of my mouth. Insects, hookworms, tapeworms. Potential tenants for my small intestine.

Try to get back to the thread of the conversation. "Freelance, yeah . . ."

"Decimal. Look. Look at me."

To the best of my ability I look at her. I think of Kali, goddess of annihilation. Maybe that's racist, just cause she's part Indian or Pakistani or whatever.

"You're about to die right here, unless you tell me where the box and the girl are."

I don't remember why I shouldn't tell her. So I do. Well, half of it anyway.

"The box. The one with the haunted-house hand in it? It's in the trunk. In, in my briefcase. Just take it. The woman is at my place, the Main Branch Public Library. Don't want any more trouble out of you all, do what you have to do."

She stares at me. Kali the Destroyer. "I believe you." She aims the .45 at my face and cocks the hammer.

Nothing I can do about it. I prepare to get shot. Keep my eyes open at least. Fuck her, fuck you, and fuck everything.

The gunshot comes from above and to the right.

Anne whips her head to the left, then forward, *plop*, straight into the dirt.

It takes me a moment or two, but it becomes clear that Anne has been shot, not me. Blood snakes out the side of her head, darker and brighter than her hair.

I'm not making connections as quickly as I'd like, having just had my skull pounded on. I'm very tired. Reach in my pocket. Thank God, the key's still there.

Someone or something is coming down the embankment, I sense this but the curtain is falling. The last thing I'm aware of is being lifted up, and a familiar voice. I get the notion that I have permission to black out.

So I black out.

Looking at a white plastic digital clock/radio. 6:18 a.m. flips over to 6:19. My body hurts, and when I say this I mean it hurts everywhere. Where are my pills?

Wait for details to come back to me. None are forthcoming. I am under some sort of plush comforter, on sheets with unquestionably the highest thread count I have ever laid my skinny chassis on. I smell cigarette smoke. Reminds me that I like to smoke as well. Reminds me . . .

I lift my head, which is more difficult than it sounds, and peer over the bedding, past my feet.

"Well, you're alive," says Iveta Shapsko. She's in a white terry-cloth bathrobe, legs tucked under her, sitting on a sofa chair next to a floor-to-ceiling window. Her hair is up in a towel. Knocks the head off her cigarette into a black glass ashtray to her right. "You, you are lucky bastard."

I try and fail to speak.

"Must be a lot of pain."

I croak, a single syllable.

Iveta takes a drag, inhales it sharply. "There was many things to clean up. You were like complete mess."

She points her cigarette toward the corner of the room. I follow her gesture to the pile of bloody towels, my discarded clothing, bunches of duct tape, gauze streamers, and a pair of bolt cutters. Broken handcuffs, the leg bracelet in two pieces.

"Told you I was a nurse. Maybe you have internal bleeding but I don't think so. I would get MRI. For your head. You seem to know the right people to get this first-class treatment."

I lift up my arm, hurts like hell, bandaged up, thick layers of gauze and duct tape on my forearm.

"You insist. Remember? *Get this thing out of me!* Waving your arm in my face. Then you pass out again, I don't know what I'm looking for. So, I dig around. Should be okay."

She crushes the cigarette. Smiles.

"Don't worry, I threw this chip out, somewhere on West Side Highway, near these Chelsea Piers I think."

I can't manage to articulate anything.

"Saw this leg thing, yes, it's tracking device too. And I think maybe you want it off, right? I will throw it away, later."

Iveta yawns. I can't get my mouth to behave. She cracks her knuckles.

"Okay, you rest more. Me, I'm tired too. Long night."

She gets up, takes the towel off her hair and scratches her damp scalp. Looks at her nails for a second. Standing there in the robe. Then she moves over to the bed, hops in, rolls over with her back facing me. Her hair follows gravity and I'm looking at that mole again.

"It's okay," she says, sounding exhausted. "It's safe, this place. I must sleep, you should too. Okay, just to rest, for a few minutes . . ." Iveta trails off.

I have serious questions. Plenty of questions. But I can hardly move my jaw. I don't think I can sleep, but

I close my eyes, listen to the pattern of Iveta's light breathing.

It's music, like rain.

The elevator. The hallway. The key. The shot.

I jerk awake. Well, my fragmented consciousness. Can't say it's not predictable.

I've been dozing for some time, must have, cause it's midafternoon. I look over at the women in bed with me.

Iveta fucking Shapsko.

The job has taken on a life of its own, an intelligence. It's sprouted legs, up and gone run off.

Ease myself to a seated position. I'm in a pair of underwear. My legs and stomach are a Jackson Pollock of cuts, bruises, welts, and old scars. My android's kneecap. My midsection is wrapped tight. Breathing hurts.

Push off from the bed, move toward the window. I'm looking at a bird's-eye of the Freedom site. My stomach drops instinctively.

I must be in the Millennium Hotel. A slick ebony binder on the leather-padded desk confirms this.

Heading to the bathroom. I pause and look at Iveta as she sleeps, sleeping hard, her mouth open and mashed against the pillow. Communicating something to me, communicating surrender, communicating complete trust. Trust I certainly have not earned, quite the opposite.

And yet, here she lies.

She's so many steps ahead of me in this particular game. I need to know what she knows, that she can release herself so completely.

How long has it been since I've shared a bed with anyone? Couldn't even say. Have I shared a bed with someone who recently shot me? Not lately.

I hobble into the bathroom, feeling like somebody's stabbing me in the liver . . . There's a half-full bottle of rubbing alcohol next to the free soaps, as well as some iodine. Fresh rolls of gauze.

My green box cutter is in a drinking glass with the hotel logo on it, soaking in pinkish liquid. I wince at the sight, but retrieve the box cutter.

Iveta's clothes are in a heap on the floor. Jeans, a T-shirt and light black cardigan, sensible bra and white underpants. A pair of New Balance sneakers.

Under normal circumstances, New Balance running shoes would be a dealbreaker for me, on a lady. Yeah, I'm snobby like that. But in Iveta's case, it somehow makes her all that much . . . more. Like she doesn't even need to try.

Take a piss and wash my face, scrub it with the alcohol. I look exhumed. Both eyes are black, likely my nose is broken, as well as a cheekbone. Bandages and tape cover my ears. I don't study this in detail. And I'm wearing a gauze turban where my hat should be.

Speaking of turbans, I contemplate this particular hotel for a second. Nowadays, the Millennium is reserved for the legion of workers involved with the Freedom Tower project, which of course saw a setback last February when it was, well, blown up. The upper floors, where we seem to be, judging by my look out the window, are reserved for the money guys, the sheiks, the Saudis.

The original Freedom Tower project, by the way, included repairs to the Islamic center and that massive mosque, so nobody could say the money people were taking sides.

As we learned, it was never that simple anyway.

The Saudis, who also own the Millennium itself, have been undeterred by the disaster, and are pressing forward. Of all construction sites and crews, they seem to be the best funded, are making swift progress; and beyond that I know nothing about them. Except that they're working with private money and aren't part of the federal Great Reconstruction program.

The only reason I can recount even that much is that there was a brief media to-do where a prominent (Republican, natch) senator tried to get the plug pulled on the project, her point being something like it was Saudi money and Saudi men who helmed those planes, way back in September 2001, so how could we in good conscience allow them to take ownership of this property, etc. But nobody seemed comfortable with that kind of thing, this type of thinking being out of vogue; and anyway, it was soon overshadowed by bigger stories.

Why I can remember trivia like this and cannot conjure up simple facts about my own life, this is beyond my understanding.

Regardless. I limp out of the bathroom, clock Iveta's black Reebok sports bag . . . and my briefcase, phew . . . and my suit jacket, sitting with the bloody towels. It's pretty well fucked, to say nothing of the pants, which are unspeakably screwed. My heart in my throat, I plunge my hand into the front pants pocket. Okay, the key is where it should be. For now I hold it in my fist.

Goddamn, this was my last suit.

I sigh and shake down the jacket, hearing the dulcet percussion of pills hitting plastic bottle. At least I had that much foresight, put the pills in my pocket . . . Can you imagine, had I not?

Retrieving these babies, I take one, cupping my hands under the water faucet and drinking. Again I douse my hands with the rubbing alcohol.

I go back out and take another gander: briefcase, check. Shoes, check. Kevi vest, check. My hat. Fantastic.

Iveta must've gone over the car pretty thoroughly. My shoulder holster is on the floor, complete with guns. All good news.

I register the keycard, sitting on the desk, a pair of cards. I grab one. Then I pick up the severed leg-bracelet, pull another fluffy bathrobe out of the closet near the door, and slide into it. I'm lost in the thing, it dwarfs me. I pull the sash tight, gasping in pain as I constrict my rib area. I loosen it and drop the key in the robe pocket, making a mental note to not leave it behind.

Exit as quietly as possible so as not to wake Iveta. The *Do Not Disturb* sign is already hanging off the exterior handle.

I'm back in less than ten minutes.

Recalling the fact that the hotel has an open-air restaurant, I took the stairs down to the twelfth floor. Walked straight through the place, head held high, Central American staff gawking but nobody saying shit. I tried to vibe Saudi. Got to the edge of the balcony and threw the ankle bracelet as far as I could manage. It cleared the fence and landed within the construction site near some yahoos in hard hats standing around bullshitting. I ducked out before they could look up.

Back to the stairwell, decided I just couldn't do it, actually hailed the elevator, took a deep breath, and rode it back to our floor.

Baby steps. I'm working on it.

Iveta is up when I get back to the room. Sitting in bed, smoking, the TV is on BBC with the sound muted. It's a rerun, they're all reruns, the G20 meeting is happening in Toronto. When was that, 2010?

"Just now, I ordered coffee for both of us," she says, smiling at me and closing her robe tighter.

"That sounds perfect." My voice is hoarse as hell, did I get kicked in the throat? Not that I recall.

Where do I begin? "I'm rather amazed," I say.

"About what?"

"You worked hard to keep me alive here. Could've left me for dead, I would have understood."

She shrugs."Only fair. Consider what you did for me."

"What are you talking about?"

She puts out her cigarette, has another poised and ready. "I know at least two people who want me to disappear. Maybe three. And I know you have been in contact with all of them. I can assume only you have been protecting me."

"How do you figure that?"

"You knew my location, you did not come after me, and you must have misdirect others so I could not be found."

I think: is that really what I did? Maybe a little bit.

"That's perceptive. I hadn't thought about it but I reckon you're on the right track."

She tilts her head. "What are reasons for this? I'm

sure these men told you terrible, nasty things I have done. That I am this dangerous person. I don't know what they said. But why not believe them?"

"I don't know what to believe. Also, I was, I am, curious. About you."

Iveta lights the new cigarette, waves the match out and drops it in the ashtray. "Curious, curious how?"

I lower myself into the sofa chair. "When people come to me and want to . . . okay, disappear someone, I want to know why. Just generally. And I want to know why it is that they can't just do it themselves. If they have solid reasoning, that they can demonstrate, then that's one thing. If not, well . . ."

I shift in my seat, trying and failing to get remotely comfortable. My ass hurts. And sometimes honesty . . . well. Hurts too.

"You know, I may come off like a psychopath but I do have a System, a kind of moral code."

Iveta smokes, looking past me out the window. "I shot you."

"In the knee. It was a tactical move. You could have gone for a kill shot, you would have been well within your rights, you know that. I can tell you have training."

She lifts her shoulders in a noncommittal gesture.

"And I did break into your house and threaten you and your son . . ."

"True," she says.

"Which makes me think, where is the kid? Where's Dmitri?"

"London. Rather, in transit. Stay with my sister, it's better. Don't want him in the middle, be used like hostage."

"How could you have possibly gotten him on a trans-Atlantic flight?"

"I have a friend in D.C., working at the embassy for Latvia. I call her, it's easy."

"And you didn't go with him."

"Are you disappointed?" She smiles. "No. I have no travel documents, you see, so I cannot get anywhere. Everything is with Yakiv . . . Lucky, I had Dmitri's papers at this house in Queens." She takes a drag, lets it out slow. "Besides. So much to do here."

"Yeah?" I say.

There's a soft knock at the door.

"That's coffee," says Iveta. "Do you mind?"

While Iveta is showering (again) and changing in the bathroom, I get a hankering for a cigarette. Pat down my jacket. No cigarettes. Keep forgetting. But: three sheets of awkwardly folded paper in the inner pocket . . . Trump letterhead?

Oh yeah, the list of residents at the Trump Tower. Courtesy of who's-that-kid . . . Reginald the doorman, for whom I wish only the best things.

I see Iveta's pack of cigarettes, grab one. With a menthol between ring and forefinger, I get back to my coffee. I'm really hungry, I realize.

Spread the crumpled paper out. Might as well have a look. Humming as I go down the list. *A, B, C* . . . Toward the end: *Rosenblatt, Daniel*. Number 1119.

Immediate knot in my stomach.

I light the cigarette, hand shaking a bit. Check on my key, still present. I memorize: apartment number 1119.

It used to be you'd throw a rock in this town and hit a Jew. Less so these days.

District Attorney Daniel Rosenblatt. Same man? My gut says absolutely yes. How could it not be, given this wacky job?

I fold up the papers, slide them into my pocket. I don't have a clue what this means in the larger scheme. But. Still.

This is a rough call, but I fetch my pistol.

Iveta emerges in a minute or so, fully dressed. Sits

down across from me, takes her cup with two hands. Like a girl.

"I'm cold. Too much AC."

She's got flecks of blood on the front of her T-shirt. My blood. Small spatters of red and brown decorate her jeans and sweater.

I show her the gun. Direct it at her.

Iveta flinches. Then rolls her eyes, uncoils. Sits back, arms folded. "You must be fucking kidding. Again?"

"Not kidding."

"Okay, what is this problem now? I thought we had become friends, Mr. Decimal."

"Yeah, I kinda did too." I won't lie, it's not easy to be pointing a gun at this woman. But I say, "Tell me about DA Daniel Rosenblatt."

She goes very still. That right there, that more or less tells me the story. "You . . . know him?"

"Obviously not well enough. But yeah. He's my occasional employer."

I can see the gears turning as Iveta chews on this new factoid. "Well . . . this, this is a big coincidence."

"Is it?"

"Daniel was very kind to me and to my child." She takes a sip of coffee. Casual, cool.

"Yeah? That's a lovely picture."

"He told you about us?"

"Not exactly."

"Then how do you—"

"This is where you went, the Trump, after leaving me at your house. Right?"

"Yes, but I thought you knew this. Not about me and Daniel. About where I am staying."

"I had an idea. But I only confirmed it for myself yesterday evening."

"So, perhaps you were not protecting me at all then."

"That's not what I'm saying. I had plenty of opportunities to give you up, I just didn't do it. Seemed wrong. I don't know who anybody is. I'm playing darts in the dark here."

"Playing . . . ?"

"Never mind. What I'm saying is I'm not sure whose side I'm on cause everybody is tossing bullshit at me and I'm running myself ragged trying to figure you people out."

Iveta scratches her neck. "If you have to know."

"I think that would begin to put me at ease here."

I recommit myself to training the pistol on her. Like I said, not easy. She searches my face. Sighs.

"Daniel and me, we had very big fight. Really bad. Just last night, before I saw you. He went crazy. Said he had 'new information.' About me. Said he would turn me in to these authorities—with no papers I would be in big shit."

"Gosh, I'm sorry to hear that." I hate my tone. I sound like a bitchy girlfriend. "But you understand, Iveta, there's just too many fucked-up connections here for my taste. I start to get the sense that everybody's talking to everybody else and the overall plan is to fuck with my skull."

She shakes her head. "This world does not revolve around you. Okay, I'll tell you. About Daniel and me. Do you want to hear? Maybe not?"

Keeping the gun up, I shake out another of Iveta's smokes one-handed. I hate menthols. "Yeah, let's hear it."

She stares at me for a bit. "You think I'm lying to

you? Mister, you have big fucking ego, I tell you this. Okay, understand. You're my only hope here. Do you understand that much?"

What is she telling me?

I pick up the matches, they say *Trump Tower*. Fold one down and snap my fingers, light up. Party trick.

But I gotta admit, I'm distressed. I don't like me, not like this. Forget for a second why I'm holding the gun. Oh yeah.

I push forward. "I'm your only hope. If you say so, darling. You're up shit's creek in that case, cause I don't have the best track record when it comes to taking care of people."

"I doubt that. Also, like I said, with Daniel, it is over. I'm afraid of him. He's insane."

"He's a douche bag. A cream puff."

"You sound like jealous husband."

I scoff at that shit. But she's right. "Please. Daniel Rosenblatt? He's got nothing going on save his title. Otherwise he's just a squirrel trying to get a nut. A little man. Bottom-feeder."

"No, really he is dangerous. Very dangerous. To me, to you."

I wait. Trying to decide if I should pocket the gun. I don't want to be doing this.

She looks at her nails. They're cut short. Seems to make a decision. "This trouble I had, in Riga . . ."

"Yeah?"

"It's not good at all. I was very young. Stupid, you know. Was part of this political student group. Do things like, small things, making statues explode, bomb threats on public buildings."

"Doesn't sound so bad. Dudes I knew in high school . . ."

"Well. I had trained as nurse and was working at Latvian military hospital. Anyway. After work hours, I let some comrades in through, what is it, a service door, they plant explosives in basement. I had no idea about the explosives, I thought . . . simple vandalism or something. Like a symbol. I was wrong. Explosives went off and kill six people."

Huh. "Jesus."

Iveta nods. "I know. It's not good. This is why I left the country. If I go back there, I go to jail or worse. Daniel knows this, and he would use it. He would deport me, no problem."

This sounds a bit off. "How could Daniel possibly know this stuff?"

"I told him. Some of it."

"Why?"

"I trusted him. Like I am telling you now. And then he gets this 'new information,' I don't know what it says."

"Uh-huh. It just, it seems to me he's too much of a pussy to do something so extreme."

"Extreme? He is ordering executions. God knows what else. I'm frightened of Daniel like I am frightened of Yakiv."

"Who is a killer and a rapist, right?"

"Yes. You don't believe me about Yakiv. He charmed you, huh? He's very charming, sure."

"I don't believe anybody at the moment," I say, and I mean it. Though fuck knows, if I want to believe anybody, she's sitting right in front of me.

Then Iveta does a crazy, reckless thing. Leans forward, softly places her hand over mine. My hand that holds the pistol.

My stomach rises and flips. I stiffen up and immediately am thinking about Purell™. On instinct. Then I'm thinking about her hand, her skin. Rougher than I expected. That's not a bad thing.

She holds my gaze. Calm. Says, "Mr. Decimal. Look at me. I'm just a person. You say I saved your life last night. Okay. You maybe save mine over last few days. I need you to at least try and hear me."

I don't say anything. I like the fact that Iveta is touching me, holding the hand that holds the gun. I like the idea of it. The idea of her.

"But I won't be threatened by you anymore," she says. "I don't think you want it like this either."

Right. Cause there's a piece that doesn't fit in this configuration, hand on hand on gun. It's the gun. The gun doesn't fit.

I lower my hand to the table. Iveta maintains eye contact and doesn't let go.

Very gently, I remove the Beretta with my other hand and place it on the glass.

Then it's just us, just the hands.

But it's too much, so I pull it away, gradually, but I pull away.

I nod at her. Lean back and feel a fuck of a lot better.

"Are you okay?" she asks.

Nod again. Weirdly, I feel myself choking up, but I nip that shit right in the bud. There will be none of that.

"Okay, I tell you," says Iveta Shapsko.

Iveta saying, "First, I am a survivor." She's smoking now. Takes a moment to look at the cigarette. "Always, I survive. I had this big problem in Riga. Joined NATO army, went to Bosnian conflict. Trouble there too. When I met Yakiv in Odessa, he was a powerful man. Had been in Serbia, like me. Over there, everyone needs protection. Especially women. See what I mean?"

I'm with her. Can't describe the relief, with the gun out of the picture.

"Not great situation, for women. This sex trade, within Ukraine and across borders. All over the world." She picks up her coffee, puts it back down. "Yakiv will take me to America, easy for him, he has already this, what is it, network. So I come in with other girls. Easy."

I'm hearing her. I wonder if she was offended when I took my hand away. But I can't read this woman.

She says, "Then Yakiv and I became close. In the way that you do, the same experience. Like this. It made it easier . . ." She looks down for a moment, then continues. "It made it easier to look over the things he did, before. In Serbia, in Ukraine. Like a monster. But I need him, so I say past is past."

I get it. I nod.

"So, time, it moves fast or it moves slow, but it moves. Things become difficult. We are fighting, all the time. At this embassy party, I meet Daniel. Now, I am in situation where I need to get away from Yakiv. Daniel, he is not handsome, he is not funny, but he is powerful in the way that Yakiv was back home. Like I said, I am a survivor. Yakiv went off this night with his friends and probably some whores. So I let Daniel seduce me. Why not? I need American protection in America, not fucking crap machismo Slav protection."

This is hard to hear. I say, "Rosenblatt is a . . . Rosenblatt is a bad guy. Orders hits, shakedowns, skims drug profits—whatever smells like money, he's into it." I should know, right?

Iveta gives me a look. "You think I'm a teenager? I know this. And you too, you know this, because you're one of his, how do you say it, one of his tools."

To which I respond: "That's not how I'd describe it. I think a better word would be *pawn*. And fuck that. I work for myself. Not anybody else. We have that in common, I am a survivor too—first, foremost, and always."

"But Daniel, he hired you to . . . hit Yakiv. Is this not true?"

Since we're having this little talk, might as well be straight. "Well. Yeah. True."

"So why is Yakiv not disappearing? Are you not very good at this job?"

Woah now. Feelings and touching and grooving on shit is one dimension, but I don't like to have my qualifications questioned. "Look here, lady, I told you that I don't like to harm anyone until I'm clear on the reasons why I'm doing so."

"I can give you plenty of these reasons for Yakiv."

"Funny, that's kind of what he had to say about you."

"And of course Yakiv is the respectable businessman. Why not accept what he says?"

"I don't. I'm reserving my conclusions."

Iveta looks at me hard. "And Daniel, he hired you to kill me as well, do you deny this?"

Okay, I could play this one of two ways. I wrack my brain for a good reason to say yes. I want to say yes. But I say: "No, that's one thing he did not do. In fact, looking back on it, he went out of his way to keep me away from you. Guess the flame still burns in old Daniel's black heart. That's kind of sweet, isn't it?"

"Oh stop it. Like I say, there was a time when he was very good to me."

"I don't doubt it. He's been good to me too. Always with an agenda. No, in fact, the DA didn't engage me to kill you. That was your husband."

She looks confused for a split second, then shrugs. "Yes, that makes sense. Why not? So. Hit man. Tough guy. You are waiting to see who has the best story before you make your moral decisions."

"Something like that."

Iveta Shapsko leans forward. No makeup, no nothing, in dirty clothes, and she is distracting in her beauty.

"Well then, I have some fantastic stories about your new best friend Mr. Yakiv."

Through fucking around, I'm headed north on the 1 train to the Maritime.

In case it all goes to shit, I booked another room back at the Millennium, just adjacent to ours, under the named Donny Smith.

I made damn sure I stuck the briefcase in there, the mummified hand of mystery very much on my mind. And Iveta. Told her to sit tight, lock the door. Just in case.

Made sure I had: key, pills, box cutter, plastic baggie, Purell™, and a little Maglite. Thought about taking the briefcase with me, decided against it. See, I can demonstrate a little trust every now and then too.

Monday, just past "rush hour" . . . so there's two other individuals in the subway car with me, and they're TA cops. I try not to make eye contact. My guns weigh heavy on me, and I'm relieved as always to get the hell out of their company when I disembark at 14th Street.

It was a cinch to get a new suit and I'm happy about that. Through a broken window at Century 21, straight to the men's department . . . I gave myself a max time limit of ten minutes, tough to shop by flashlight but it is what it is. I finally settled on a pinstripe Paul Smith job that I could never have afforded in pre–2/14 conditions. I figure I'm worth it.

My shoes are still holding up.

Collected some extra underwear, socks, a couple shirts, bingo, it's the new me.

On impulse, I grabbed a lovely Marc Jacobs dress for Iveta. I didn't analyze this action, I just did it. She took it, and said it was lovely.

So I come up out of the underground with a heart full of thick fucking hate, which is going to be essential to my task ahead.

This is great; usually I don't have a vibe one way or the other, and this makes me unfocused.

Yakiv is a goddamn animal. No, in fact it's an affront to animals the world over to call him an animal. There's no descriptor strong enough for this person. The laundry list of atrocities I got from Iveta challenges human comprehension. There is not a vile action that my pal Yakiv hasn't engaged in, short of cannibalism. And even there, though . . . an occasion related to me when he made a Russian mafioso boss, at gunpoint, eat his own daughter's heart, after she died during a brutal gang rape in which Yakiv participated, which said Russki mobster was forced to witness.

In Serbia he slaughtered entire towns. Everyone dead. But not before they'd been systematically raped (women, men, children) and made to carry out the duty of digging their own graves. It was a highly structured operation, meticulous.

So no more fucking around, Decimal.

What he did to Iveta I hope to never hear about again, and I will never repeat it. Never.

All this propels me west on 14th Street. One block to Ninth Avenue, two blocks to the hotel. I'm so amped, I almost don't notice the goddamn Stench. Almost.

Dig me now. My approach is System-based and sound in its logic.

I cross over Ninth Avenue, and between 15th and 16th I have a look at the doors to the old Chelsea Market. Locked, but somebody has created an improvised entryway leading into that mediocre Italian place by knocking out all the glass in one of the doors. So it's accessible.

I ditched the turban of gauze in favor of my hat, and if you don't look too closely at my face, which is alarmingly re-organized despite Iveta's makeup treatment, I pass for a freakin class act.

Very pleased with the suit, I'm going to have to remember this Paul Smith fellow for future reference. My key sits well in the deep pants pocket.

Got my vest on, and guns good to go.

First I walk around front and observe that there is a single man stationed at the stairs leading to the restaurant balcony. Just happens that I glance up Ninth Avenue on the west side of the street, and I stop cold.

Hold the phone.

A Lincoln Navigator, black, tinted windows . . . but surely . . .

Surely there can't be just the one Navigator in town? After all, this spot is VIP central. If there's Navis anywhere, they'd be concentrated here. I can tell myself this, but I slip closer, just outside of the lights of the Maritime.

The Navigator is seemingly unoccupied. Move closer still. Close enough to savvy the red, white, and blue plates that tell me . . . what? Branko's here? I've still got the tail? This adds up to . . . ?

I can't do the math. But it gives me a new idea, a new angle. Might clear out some cobwebs. Proceed. It's on.

Back around the side entrance of the Maritime, I take

the stairs two at a time, past the footmen, projecting *I belong*, visualizing it, owning it.

Nobody says a word despite that fact that I'm a black dude, which is generally grounds enough to get kicked out of anywhere white people want to actually relax. Into the lobby, which is a little more on the muted side tonight, less pumping party action going down on a Monday evening. Couples get intimate across complex-looking frozen drinks.

I note several black-suited hulkers with that telltale coiled gray cord coming out of their collars and into their earpieces. Three guys, positioned near the entrance to the elevator banks, at the neon blue–lit bar, and next to the side stairwell leading to 16th Street.

I picture the pattern I would employ to take them all out, an easy 360-degree swing to the left, *boom, boom, boom.*

Approach the desk. An "attractive" blonde surgically altered to the extent that she joins that subspecies of humans that no longer look like anything, except that they've had a lot of plastic surgery, and therefore all look strangely like the same person.

"Can I be of service?"

Russian accent, "bee-stung" lips looking painfully swollen to the point of bursting. Skin over skull pulled tight, tight, tight. Poor thing, she was once a beautiful little baby. Her visage is distracting in exactly the opposite way Iveta distracts.

"Yes, Branko Jokanovic here to see Yakiv Shapsko."

She frowns, which stretches things even tighter. Only her mouth moves. It's disturbing. "We have no such person here. Perhaps you are mistaken?"

Boring. I lower my voice. "Listen, cupcake, I truly

shudder at the thought of the punishment Yakiv would dole out on your silicone if he knew you were holding up our meeting."

She looks taken aback . . . I imagine. I'm extrapolating because her face doesn't move, can't move.

"I was here with him two nights ago, you saw me. Get him on the phone. The name is Branko Jokanovic. I work for Yakiv's attorney."

She now has her hand on the phone. This is going to work. "Lawyer?" she says doubtfully, as if testing out the word.

"That's what I said, bon-bon, so go ahead, call him, that's a good girl. Branko Jokanovic, the name, all you gotta do is tell him I'm here and we're done."

Svetlana or whatever the fuck her name is hesitates a few moments longer, casts her eyes at the lobby muscle who stand oblivious, thinking about whatever those guys think about when they're standing around. Then she picks up the receiver and taps out a sequence of numbers, her nails pornographically long.

I'm being tough on her, but plastic surgery in any amount just makes me want to puke. Call me judgmental, but it indicates a certain set of accompanying goals, fashion choices, and behaviors. It's trashy and it means you don't like yourself.

Tell me I'm wrong.

"Mr. Shapsko, please." She's speaking in Russian, which suits me fine.

We wait. And wait. She doesn't look at me, which also suits me fine.

"Branko Jokanovic," I repeat. She holds up a finger. I hate when people do that.

I do a head count. Maybe fourteen couples and four singles in the bar. Plus the three security guys and two teenagers in the Mao jackets. Hope I don't have to waste civilians, that would be tragic. On the other hand, if they're hanging here, they're probably into some bad shit.

"Yes, this is the front desk."

I return my attention to the receptionist. She's an absolute vision. A deeply disturbing vision.

"I am so sorry to disturb you. I have a person calling himself Branko Jokanovic downstairs? If you wish, I will have security remove . . ." She pauses. "No, I'm quite sure, Branko Jokanovic. Shall I have him removed?"

I suddenly feel a rush of sympathy for this person. I've been assuming things. Like the fact that the plastic surgery was her choice. I know that when people assume shit about me, I don't like it.

Clearly, Yakiv is now chewing her out; she looks at the floor. I know the kind of control mechanisms these guys deploy. If you're a sixteen-year-old girl and you fall in with such men, it's all over. Where this puts you when you're on the wrong side of thirty has to be grim.

What's wrong with me? I'm all over the place, gotta focus.

She places the receiver down carefully. Says, "Mr. Shapsko is on his way here." Doesn't make eye contact.

In our last moments together I want to take it all back. "Miss," I say in Russian, "I apologize for being rude. That was uncalled for. Had a bad day at work and I took it out on you a little bit. I wish only the best for you and your family." It comes out very formal—what can I say, my Russian is textbook.

She looks at me, head cocked. "Fine. You can wait in

the bar." In English. Icy chilly. She's got that thick skin. Fair enough. She'll need it.

I thank her and mosey over to the bar, my plan all along, dropping my skinny ass on a black and chrome stool. It's like architecture and design got stuck on auto repeat in the 1990s.

I position myself as far toward the street as possible. The balcony is open. To get to me, the thugs would have to walk two abreast maximum, probably single file. All according to plan.

Bartender plops a coaster (*Stolichnaya Vodka*) in front of me. "What are we drinking this evening?" He's a short guy with black hair, thick eyebrows.

I decide what the hell, treat myself. "We are drinking a Shirley Temple. Hold the cherry." Nasty-ass maraschinos.

Dude blanks me.

"You know, like Sprite or 7UP with some grenadine syrup? You don't get any kids in here?"

"For no alcohol, we have bottled water."

No fun. "That'll work."

He disappears, I'm watching the elevator bank. The heavy nearest me just outside the bar is talking into his headset, he does an unsuccessfully casual turn and clocks me, starts talking again.

I look to the right. Yeah, all the muscle is chatting. They're on standby. I swivel to my left and check the balcony, hand in pocket. Dinner is being served but they're thin on clientele. I run my finger across the edge of my key.

As far as I can see, no security out there, save the dude down the stairs on Ninth Avenue. Mustn't forget about him.

Bust out some Purell™, lather up. Ready as I'll ever be. Adrenaline kicks in and this feels grand.

Yakiv comes out of the elevator, flanked by two more sides of beef.

The bartender deposits my water in front of me. Quickly, I down a pill and chase it.

Yakiv heads for the front desk, but one of the men touches his shoulder and indicates me. I wave. Howdy-do. His face goes through several stages, initially amusement, then momentary befuddlement, then straight-up anger.

He's coming toward me. And, hail Lucifer, he must've told his men to relax, because he's beelining my direction on his lonesome. The heavy in front of the bar steps aside as Yakiv passes. He's adjusting his face into an approximation of cool. But the man is pissed.

"This name," he's saying. "Why do you use this name, you think that is fucking funny?" Gets right up in my face. I put up my hands, placating. I feel a collective tensing of muscle throughout the room.

"Woah, Yakiv, cool it down. Yeah, it was a joke, just trying to keep you frisky. Don't want to get soft, right? Hey, is Branko here? I ask cause I did notice his car just out front . . ."

"Not fucking funny. And not funny to remove leg bracelet. I think this is not working out. Huh?" Yakiv gestures to his guys.

"You're wrong there, friend. I did the job."

"Bullshit," he says, face going red again.

Okay, I need to make my move soon. "Iveta. Done. I have photographs . . ." I reach into my jacket, the room rushes forward, but not before I've spun Yakiv around, established a headlock, and jammed the Sig Sauer in his ear.

"Back the fuck up!" I tell the collective hunks in Russian.

Brief chaos. People duck under tables, the bar clears out fast. Gives me a moment to get a really solid hold on Shapsko. The man saying, "Oh, this is a really big problem for you. Really big."

The muscle looks to Yakiv. Their weapons are out. Something of a rush, having seven or eight guns pointed at you. Their problem: the narrow opening to the bar, a low wall really, creates a bottleneck effect.

Yakiv sounds almost bored, speaks Russian: "Hang on a moment, men, let's see how this unfolds."

"Yeah, hang on a moment, fellows," I say, also in my schoolbook Russian. "Come closer, I shoot your boss. Or maybe I'll just cripple the man so he can remember which one of you blew it for him."

I'm thinking about the guy at the bottom of the balcony stairs. I don't see the dude, which I take to mean they want him to remain there. Wise.

Everybody's jawing into their earpieces.

We start backing up, out onto the balcony.

"Yakiv," I whisper into his ear, "I know what you are. I know what you've done. See? You're not going to make it tonight, this is it for you."

We continue backing up. If the guy comes up the stairs I might be fucked, so I start to move faster before anybody on a 'com figures that out as well.

Yakiv is actually grinning. "It's sad to me that you've been so easily made like a puppet. You're in the middle of something you don't understand. You have the story completely confused. Iveta, she will eat you alive."

"Just hush-a-bye. You're not doing yourself any good."

Still backing up. I see two of the guys inside make a run for the side entrance. Ah, they're going to go around the side of the building. Smart stuff.

We are about to round the stairs where we will probably be met by more security. I put pressure on Yakiv's carotid artery, cutting off his air and blood flow. I do it hard. I give it about twenty seconds, his people just straining to do something, anything, it's enough to make the man woozy. I then step backward.

Sure enough, there's the heavy at the head of the stairs, as expected. I feel confident I can take the gun away from Yakiv's head long enough to put a cap into this guy, whose mouth is one big SpaghettiO.

Do it, just as he's raising his gun, *boom*, a touch to the right of his nose. His face explodes, the sap falls backward, and I return the gun to Yakiv's temple. At the gunshot, his men inside the hotel start yelling shit, but they don't have a good move if they want to avoid clipping their boss.

Reckon it's time to cut out, while I'm enjoying a slight leg-up. I pull Yakiv down the stairs, and once we clear the line of sight with his men, I can hear them scrambling in our direction.

Halfway down the block, two of Yakiv's guys come around the corner, the smarter of the two immediately ducking back behind the building, the dumber half raising a pistol and jogging our way like a moron.

I take careful aim from behind Yakiv's shoulder and fire, first shot going wide, shit, fire again and he clutches his thigh and goes down midskip, skids to a stop on the pavement. Shoot him once more so he doesn't continue to be a problem, then turn around to face the larger grouping of men who are taking up position along the balcony's edge. They're dying to open up, I can't blame them, but they're just not getting a decent look at me.

I'm concerned with the fellow to my right, hanging tough around the corner. I can't use Yakiv as a shield in two different directions simultaneously.

The Ukrainian has recovered from the Vulcan neck-grip and is doing his best to drag his feet and generally make it difficult for me to move.

"Brilliant plan," he says. "You must be very proud."

"Tell them to stand down," I say.

Yakiv just smiles.

"I said, tell them to chill and back up."

The man says nothing of the kind. And of course he's playing his cards right, I expect that if I shoot him I'd find myself in a downpour of bullets. The only power I wield at the moment is conditional on Yakiv being alive.

I sigh. Okay, we'll just take it as it comes.

Set out across Ninth Avenue, backward, angling south. This seems to be working. One step at a time. Yakiv takes this moment to put his elbow in my gut, a good effort but I have the vest on.

Which is apparently what he was trying to determine. "Listen," he calls in Russian to his boys, "he's wearing a Kevlar vest. Go for a headshot. If you feel like you can take it, take it. I trust all of you like brothers."

Well played by Yakiv. Shit. I guess I shouldn't be surprised.

The guy on the street who has been waiting for just such an opportunity must be digging himself tonight, because he pops out and squeezes one off.

I duck behind Yakiv, hell yeah I do, I'm no hero, and feel that hot bullet whizz right past my right ear. An excellent shot at this distance.

Yakiv decides he doesn't like this action. That one came as close to him as it did to me. "Okay, hold it! Just hold your fire. Just hold it."

The frisky dude has for the moment forgotten that he's wide open, distracted perhaps by his commitment to take the next opportunity to cap me. It's unfortunate.

Yakiv starts to say something but I'm focused on lining up my own shot. I take it and get it in one. The guy turns sideways, I can't see his expression from here, and collapses. Some would frown on this kind of thing, but I line up another one, and for the second time I shoot a man who is already down.

Now things are considerably easier. Yakiv knows it.

"I never took you for suicidal type. This is certainly going to end poorly for you." Et cetera. Trying to psych me out but I'm past all that. He blathers on.

As we get across the street, his boys are positively jumping up and down with frustration. Half of them run inside, probably with the intention of coming around the side like their dead or dying buddies.

That's okay. I'm in the zone. I can taste it, this will work.

Dragging the Ukrainian across 16th Street now. Half a block to go, less. Yakiv is feeling my good fortune. He's trying to keep his voice relaxed and snarky but it's not coming together for him. His tone is increasingly desperate.

"Decimal, think about this, how does this end in a good way for you? You kill me, so what? You will never know things that are essential for you to stay alive. Only I can provide you this information. Okay? You only kill yourself."

I'm done talking to this man. We're like three meters from the busted-out glass door we're headed toward.

His boys arrive on the other side of the street. They're out of ideas, impotent, useless, and they're probably catching on to that themselves. They hang back as I step awkwardly over the door frame and into the dark of the dilapidated restaurant, hauling Yakiv's unwilling carcass with me.

Once we're through the doorway I step back a bit, pointing the pistol at the base of his spine. I poke him.

"Move, quick, let's go. Put your hands on top of your head. Lace your fingers."

He does as he's told. I steer him out into the main corridor that runs the length of the old Chelsea Market and terminates at Tenth Avenue. A simple maze thick with glass rooms that were once shops, bakeries, groceries, general fanciness.

All I have is the small Maglite, it'll have to do . . . I train it on the ground a couple feet in front of us as we proceed. I nudge him past the newsstand, deeper into the dark of the place. I note running water up ahead, either a leak or the fountain is somehow still functioning. Lots of broken glass litters the walkway, crunches underfoot. This place saw some pretty heavy looting.

I stop him at the old Chelsea Wine Vault on the right, the door is already busted out and we're hit with the stench of spilled, spoiled wine that has been baking in this heat for a good month and a half. It's pretty overwhelming, but I say: "In here, let's go."

He's clearly trying to come up with an angle, so indeed would I in his shoes, but the guy cooperates. "Decimal," he says as I scoot him toward the back of the shop. Broken bottles everywhere, I'm careful where I step. Dude presses on: "It's no use, this whole thing. My team will find you. Walk away right now, and I give my word as a man that no harm will come to you."

"Gosh, Shapsko, sounds like an irresistibly great deal, to which I say no." I'm playing the flashlight around on the floor near the register . . . there. A trapdoor.

See, I think I went out with this girl once who worked here. White girl. Name? That's a blank. But I am aware, somehow, that these people had a basement. Or so I seem to recall. Relieved this is not a false memory, would've made things more difficult.

"Yakiv, open that thing and climb on down."

He doesn't move. Keeping the gun on him, I lean over and pull the metal ring. The door swings free.

"Yakiv, let's go, my man."

Again he doesn't move. I flip the pistol around and come at him. He thinks I'm moving in to strike him in the head, he covers up, and I club him in the groin with the butt of my gun.

Yakiv doubles up and falls to a kneeling position. I step around him and, using my good leg, roll him into the hole. He goes bouncing down the stairs and not a second too soon, as I hear the group of thugs come stumbling into the hallway, apparently blind. I duck down into the basement staircase; when I'm partway down I turn and close the hatch gently behind me.

I shift the flashlight toward the Ukrainian. There's about two inches of black water on the basement floor.

The man is struggling with a large shard of green glass that has all but pierced his hand. Rats mill about nearby. Tough break for a proud man. He does this silently, working at the fragment, his face sweaty but concentrated. What stoicism. The problem my man contends with is that the chunk is slippery with blood and he can't pull the thing out, it's too slick. He tries it with the tail of his shirt, this fails as well.

Damn, I'm gonna need a twelve-pack of Purell™ after this foul scene.

I fetch the silencer from my jacket pocket. Roll up my pant cuffs and descend the last few steps. I go down on my haunches near him, my good knee popping. Say, "It's probably a bad idea to pull that thing out. You should know this."

Screwing on the silencer.

"Basic tenet of dealing with shrapnel. You pull the thing out, think phew, then uh-oh, you're bleeding to death. On an empty street, in some shitty building in some shitty town thousands of miles from home. Or in a fancy-pants wine cellar, wherever."

Yakiv is not meeting my eye. He's holding the glass shard, but he stops pulling at it. Not the most glamorous exit scenario for Mr. Shapsko . . . but then what would be?

"Roll over on your stomach. Let's end this thing, Yakiv."

He looks at me. Almost tenderly. "She's not who she says she is, my friend."

I start pushing him sideways with my foot.

"And neither am I," he adds.

"Oh, I'm well aware of what you are."

I kick him over. He goes facedown, lifts his head out of the filthy water, spits.

"You know me by the wrong name."

I place my foot in the small of his back. "Cryptic. I'm intrigued. Take a couple deep breaths, Yakiv, and dig on life, you're about to shuck thy mortal coil, as they say."

"Fucking joke is on you. The name you use, coming in tonight . . . shows you know nothing. And the woman you call Iveta. This woman, she cuts your throat. You are not even on her level." He sounds like he's smiling, but I'm looking at the back of his head so I'll never be sure. "You tell her I win. She never got close to me, not once. I win."

I blink. Something in what the man says . . . No.

Feel like I should lay out something clever, something about none of us being who we say we are, something big and cosmic, but I can't formulate it in a satisfying way.

So I just shoot him. Put a bullet in his neck. He starts trying to get up. Points for stick-with-it-ness. I step on him harder and plant another one behind his ear.

This time he goes limp.

I step off the man. Never what you think it's going to be. Always an anticlimax. That's the nature of murder, righteous or not.

And plus, I did kind of like the guy. Shame.

It's cold down here. As I pull away the light to guide myself up and out, I hear the raindrop pitter-patter of rats moving in.

Haste. I have another quick errand to run before I head south again.

So far as I know, there's only one proper mummy publicly displayed in New York City.

I am not surprised to find the front doors of the Metropolitan Museum of Art locked up tight. Got here quicker than anticipated; Yakiv's thugs were hopelessly on the wrong track, I could hear the boys somewhere down that dark corridor, guttural echoes, bumping into shit, -ski'ing and –vich'ing each other, digging their profound failure.

I simply sailed out the Tenth Avenue exit, problem free. Into the black air.

Took the long gimp around the back of Met, somewhat uneasy as one has to walk into the park a bit to approach the museum from the rear, with its massive sloping glass wall. Glass being the key element here.

Of course, many have beaten me to it. Post–2/14 looting started almost as soon as the Occurrence(s) themselves. Sure: this was most definitely a hot spot, folks crawling on top of each other to snag priceless bits of swag.

Obviously Yakiv and his boys had paid a visit, came out with a few truckloads of booty. Judging by his collection at the Maritime. The problem is not getting a hold of such treasure. Snatch and grab, here's a Byzantine triptych. Here's a sixteenth-century Persian death mask. Rather, the problem is unloading them. Cause who among your neighbors is in the market for a Rembrandt, or a Bronze Age chalice?

What we all realized pretty quickly: the only material of value is that which keeps us alive. Food. Water. Shelter. Weapons. Les basics.

Regardless, the joint is wide open, my predecessors having already created multiple points of entry in the breakable façade. It is a simple thing to just step inside, into that expansive hall that houses the Temple of Dendur and its reflecting pool. Rusty nickels and dimes carpeting the underwater tiles, the water green with algae.

I find the mummy by memory, trusting my memory here, crossing my fingers that nobody has fucked with it already. The mummy, I mean, not my memory. Why would they have? But still. People fuck with everything.

Looks pretty much undisturbed. The pile that had once been Chief Treasurer Ukhhotep dates from as far back as 1991 B.C., which of course is over two thousand years older than Johnny the B.

But I figure it like this: a mummy is a mummy is a mummy. It's old, dead, it's dried out. Right? How different can they be?

I produce my box cutter, rubber gloves, a large ziplock freezer bag.

And I go to work.

Sweaty but satisfied, my next stop is a quick one: Grand Central.

The main hall is a surrealist campground. Boschian. I note some expensive-looking tents, semipermanent structures, bikes, hibachis, dogs, children. There's scarcely a square meter of empty floor space.

But I bypass all this, got things to get done, head downstairs. To the self-operated storage units.

I exit via Vanderbilt Avenue. Popping a pill. Slip a keycard to a locker in my back pocket. And do up the Purell™, God knows who uses those nasty lockers.

Hang a left onto 42nd, so close to home, thinking about my books, and immediately pull myself into an atrium.

A pair of soldiers. Man, what the fuck am I thinking strutting around? No question, Rosenblatt will have put out an all-points. No question about that. I don't want to get braced by anybody in a uniform, it'd spell calamity. Game over.

And lo, here are these boy scouts, effectively blocking access to a subway. To Iveta. To some resolution.

Think fast. The grunts bullshitting, bored. Neither clocks me. One Latino kid, one black kid. Two HK MP5 machine pistols. Mad heavy firepower. Way the fuck beyond what I pack.

Come on, Decimal, work it out. Something proactive. Sick of turning tail like the weaker dog.

On the brown kid's utility belt, a portable shortwave phone.

Proactive. Think System. Simplicity.

I have it. All or nothing.

First: check for further law. East and west. Nobody, save one or two citizens.

Proactivate, Decimal.

Coming out of the recess, I drunk-stumble toward the pair. Grip my breast right-handed, like I've been cut. Hand halfway into my jacket, two inches from the butt of the Sig.

"Help," I'm slurring, the boys already facing me, at ease, sure, but both double-grip their HKs. "Fuckin . . . Gotta help, goddamn. Been robbed, man. Bitch stabbed me . . ."

The black kid holds up a hand. Other kid just hangs tight. "Let's just freeze it right there, sir . . ." Not buying this.

Stumble another foot forward, pointing now with my free arm, pointing past them, saying, "Serious, right fuckin there, the bitch has a knife . . ."

I can tell the black kid is sharp, wise to me, but: dude knee-jerk reflex follows my hand, swiveling his head, can see him gathering he blew it already, I want to console him, it's barely a moment that his attention is divided—but that's all I need.

Pray God forgives jackals such as me.

Bring my hand down now on the brown boy's Koch, other hand has the Sig out, and *boom*, I shoot my young intelligent black brother point-blank in the eye.

Pushing the Latino's HK into his groin, I take him down. He's averting his gaze, almost in embarrassment, and it's an easy thing to hit the pavement, me sitting on his gun, straddling him, the boy on his back, my Sig now shoved up under his jaw.

"Chill," I say, though he's not struggling. "Chill. Let's take a breath."

Clock his name patch. Him blinking at me.

"Diaz," I say. "Brother, I'm not gonna kill you. Your radio, that's . . ."

A tear slides out his left eye, then his right.

"Diaz, focus, man. Like I said, you're gonna walk away from this. Entiendes lo que quiero decir?"

The kid is crying. Softly. Somehow it would be preferable if he fought back.

"Okay, man," I say, trying to be mellow. "It's all gonna work out. Just want to use your radio. Let's make that happen."

"Hakim. Hakim Stanley," he says.

"Hakim . . . ?"

Diaz flips his eyes to the right. "We're from Houston, man."

"Okay," I say.

"Fuck you. Man, we was in the *sandbox* together. Two tours, not a fucking scratch, yo. And you creep up out of fucking nowhere, man." Spits in my face. "Fuck you. Fuck you if you clip me, fuck you if you don't."

I want to respond at the correct emotional pitch, really I do, but I am trying to come to terms with the fact that I have a stranger's saliva in my mouth. I'm loath to admit that this detail trumps everything at the moment. I have a real handicap . . .

Might vomit. I avert my face so as not to hurl on Diaz. Who takes the opportunity, wisely, to pull his HK up, cracking me in the mouth with its butt.

If I managed to stay my gut beforehand, the gun-to-face impact does cause me to throw up, falling sideways as I do. I'm expelling nothing but bile from my empty stomach, and I bite pavement. If I black out, it's just for a few moments. I think.

Two yards away, Diaz is methodically performing CPR on his buddy. His back to me. I'm neutralized, no longer worthy of attention.

"Diaz . . ." I say, which comes sounding like "The-ath." I put my hand to my mouth, comes away crimson.

Diaz doesn't respond. He's crouched over, listening to his buddy's decimated face. Calm like. Blow twice. Listen again.

Attempt to call to him again, can't, abort. My lips are split. I put my suit jacket sleeve to my mouth. Yet another suit; farewell, my sweet, farewell.

Listen to me. Bitching about fucking clothes.

Diaz has begun chest compressions. Pumping away. His technique is perfect, but that doesn't alter the fact that Hakim was dead before he touched ground.

Diaz switches back to the *two-breaths, listen* sequence.

I try again. "Diaz, man."

He's back at the chest compressions, vigorous. Doing everything right.

For all my self-education, for all my posturing and talk of my System, I can't escape the paradigm of my childhood, the brutal Southern Baptist duality of hard-panned extremes. The two-sided coin of pure good and of pure evil. I might be foggy on the details, but this is a stain on my spirit, and it vibes real.

Heads or tails. And I'm positive as to where I fall.

There's a special corner in Hell for the killer of children. It's extra hot. I know this like I know the contours of my Beretta.

But I never underestimate my ability to compartmentalize. I'm a genius in that department.

Bang, and Diaz is standing over me, the HK primed and shoved in my chest. Nothing to be done. It is what it is.

We lock eyes, soldier on soldier, yin and yang. The tears are history. I read resignation. To what, I don't know. I can only nod. All is as it should be.

"Do what you got to do, Diaz," I say through my teeth. Or at least think it. Sleep would be a blessing. I feel a sweet flush of . . . what? Relief.

Diaz drops his weapon. Undoes his belt. Tosses it on my chest. Removes his helmet. Steps away. I look sideways as he places the headgear over Hakim's face. He stays there for a moment, hunched over the dead kid. Lovingly, he undoes the chain around his friend's neck and palms the dog tags.

Then he's up, walking, without a backward glance.

I watch his back till I can't see him anymore. Me and Hakim, we lie there for a bit.

It's not for me to understand what just transpired. Why Diaz didn't simply pull that trigger. But in this act of not doing, the young man has transcended the situation. Shown himself to be the more radiant, vital being.

Fuck it. Let's trim the bonsais and get reflective later.

Check for the baggie and its contents. Phew. I fumble with Diaz's discarded belt. Unclip the radio. Sit up, mentally checking for further injury. Beyond my face. Spit. Clear my throat. And key in a series of nines.

"Rosenblatt," the DA picks up right away.

"Daniel," I say, pulling out some Purell™.

Staticky pause. Then, "Dead man, Decimal. You are a motherfucking. *Dead man*."

I hawk another chunk at the sidewalk. "Daniel, I'm not calling to chew fat. Calling to let you know, I'm on my way."

"Won't even. Waste *my* energy. I will *hire*. Every butcher in town. To motherfucking tear you. Limb from limb. The cunt too. Won't raise a *finger* myself. Not a *pinky*. Over here. Both of you, the *cunt*. And you, Decimal. Will *watch* her suffer. Won't be fast, *be assured*. Graphic. Sharp focus. Well lit. Follow?"

Static. Wait till I'm sure he's done. "Daniel," I say. "Fair warning. I'm coming to kill you, sir. I want you to say it, that you've heard me."

"No, *you* hear *me*. You will *wish*. You'd done her yourself. You hear *me*."

"See you soon, Daniel." Who can talk to this guy?

This time, it's me who terminates the call.

Find myself turning the corner on the eighteenth floor of the Millennium, my radar vibing bad shit.

I pause, back up around the wall. My shoes are still damp from the basement back at the Chelsea Market. Can't feel my face.

I reconfirm the key is in my front pocket and the keycard in my rear right. Wearing the radio.

Feeling hyperaware, uncomfortably so; everything is slightly too detailed, too real. I encounter this state frequently. That is, after I've killed multiple people.

Take another look down the hall. From my perspective here, it looks as if the door to our original booking is slightly ajar.

Praise Allah I got that extra room, and I hope to fuck Iveta is still in it, sitting tight. And my briefcase. The hand.

Pull my Beretta. Come around the corner and up against the far wall. Move down the carpeted hallway. I really don't want to hurt anybody else today, but so fucking help me, if Iveta is in any way endangered I'll do it happily.

Ease the door open with my gun. The lock has been jimmied in a rather ugly fashion, big gouges in the wood, the reverse end of a hammer or a crowbar.

There's an envelope, the hotel's stationary, stuck to the front door. My initials on it, *D.D.* For the moment, I leave that alone.

I can see partially into the space. It's been trashed. Hairs on the back of my neck go erect. What the hell is wrong with security up in this joint? Embarrassing.

Listen. A television, down the hall maybe. I wait for ten seconds, breathing, don't hear anything new, so I step inside.

The couch is cut up, the mattress slit straight down the middle. Air-conditioning panels have been pulled off the walls. It's a complete and total. Pillows, the leather on the desk, all slashed wide open. It's comprehensive.

I check the closet. Check the bathroom . . . chunks of porcelain cover the floor, the toilet decimated. Incredible. Whoever came through here must have had a bagful of tools.

Stepping out of the bathroom, fuck, too late, there's that nanosecond in which I sense the proximity of a human. I walk right into the barrel of another Sig Sauer.

At the end of which is Iveta.

I'm afraid she's going to pull the trigger so I'm ducking out of the way, on automatic pilot, am about to take her down, woah, check myself, I've got her around the midsection . . . She pirouettes away, lets out a torrent of gibberish, then: "Jesus, you scared me so much. Oh my god. Oh my god."

She collapses on the disemboweled couch, dropping her gun. Wearing the dress I snagged for her. Looks good in it.

"Jesus Christ. Jesus Christ. I almost shot you."

Rubbing my forehead, the veneer of sweat, I say, "Well, it wouldn't have been the first time."

"Jesus," she says, her lip trembling. "What happened to your mouth?"

"Oh. Just . . . I fell down."

Realize she's weeping. Shaking. "Tell me . . . Yakiv . . . or maybe don't tell me."

Not sure what to do. I crouch down next to her. "Okay."

She looks up at me, her face contorted, smeared. "No, tell me."

I contemplate how to put it. Not exactly sure. I just look at her.

She puts her face in her hands, shoulders bouncing up and down. Sobbing.

"Iveta . . ."

Reaching out, she grabs my hand. It's not letting up. She's got her mouth open and is just keening. It's awful. I honestly don't know what to do and I tell her this.

"Iveta, I don't know what you want me to do, what you want me to say."

We sit for a time. It starts to subside into hiccups. She has one hand pressed against her eyes. "Why am I like this? It's just . . . Okay, now it becomes real. I need. I'm sorry, there's lot of history."

"I can understand. I think."

"Don't want you to think you did this, the wrong thing."

"No, believe me. I have no doubt."

"I don't cry for him. I cry because it's all fucked and ugly."

She's gripping my hand. I'm desperately bad at this stuff. Just freeze up. Her breathing begins to slow. She laughs. It's a brittle sound.

"Sorry. I cry a lot, okay."

I think she's recovering. I try to be gentle. But like I said, I am vibing very bad shit.

"Who was here, do you have any idea?"

Shakes her head. "Don't know, it was terrifying me. They just destroy this room, look for something, I don't know what. I listened next door. So loud. I tried to call downstairs, no one answers. Oh my God, thank you for this, thinking of another room for us, I don't know what they would have done . . ."

I've got a pretty good sense of what this is all about.

"Did you see . . . on the door?" she says.

"Yeah, did you read it?"

Iveta shakes her head no. I go grab the envelope. Open it, carefully.

Hotel letterhead. Neat, small handwriting, black pen. Masculine lines, written quickly.

Attn Mr. Decimal: A Proposal

Surrender my property.
Surrender the woman.

In exchange:
Your continued good health.
Your liberty.
Your library.

Hoping for a timely conclusion to this episode.
Contact at yr earliest convenience.

Bst regards,
B. Petrovic

Ball it up, stick it in my pocket.

Iveta stirs. "Are you going to tell me?"

"Doesn't matter. Give me a second to think."

I go in the bathroom. Douse my hands in Purell™. In the shattered mirror I see Hakim Stanley, his eye a blank space, looking back at me. Mouthing, *You*. I turn my head quick, pushing the vision away . . .

"It's Daniel," she says from the other room. "Yeah? His people. I know it. He will hurt me. Best case, deport me. He said he would. They'll put me in prison."

Hot water. I grab a towel, dab at my lips. Return to Iveta, drop the towel. "Okay, get your stuff together. We gotta move."

Iveta, seated, gazes up at me, snot and tear streaked. Her eyes, damp and ocean-green. "Right now? Jesus, where do we go?"

I take out my key. It's worn and brass and nothing special, but now it all makes sense. A convergence.

The key, warm in my palm.

"Only one place jumps to mind," I say.

The 5 train is a block away, the Fulton Street station. Made positive I had the briefcase. Opened it up in the bathroom.

Downstairs I have Iveta wait by the elevators, while I scope the lobby. Don't know who I'm looking for, but I don't think I see them. The place is dead save the desk attendant, who appears to be sleeping, and a seated Saudi couple in traditional dress. As we pass by them I notice the man is reading an old issue of the *Economist*. The woman is veiled, and wears Miu Miu stiletto heels and a delicate gold ankle bracelet. Thick lashes and dark peepers clock me, slide over to Iveta in her new dress, giving her a solid once-over, that energy exchange specific to all the world's beautiful women.

Out into the evening, the burnt-plastic air. Coming up on midnight, wonder if the trains are running. Sentries are posted at the dual entrances to the 4/5, leads me to believe they're in operation. Poses problems. Can't utilize my laminate, as it's likely to get flagged. I'm sure Daniel would like to have a word at this point.

There's always the Donny Smith ID so I'd be okay, maybe, but I'm concerned about trying to run Iveta past a checkpoint. From what I've learned today, no doubt Daniel has a stop order on her as well.

No train then. We take a left off Fulton onto Broadway. Iveta is with me, quiet but watchful.

For the umpteenth time I steal a car, this one parked

in front of St. Paul's, yet another goddamn Prius. Candy apple red. Like it wants to be a sports car when it grows up.

FDR Drive down and around the bottom of the island, then all the way up to the RFK Bridge, a bridge the architects of 2/14 didn't even have on their radar because who gives a shit about people up here, right?

Clocking the rearview. A blue Nissan has been with us since the financial district. Almost certainly a tail.

Behind the Nissan, a black Navigator.

Could have been with us back downtown too. Brian and company. Another tail. A tail on the tail.

It doesn't matter, so I don't mention it.

There's a squawk of feedback. We both jump and I almost lose control of the car. Goddamn these cars, the crap handling. The radio phone, in my pocket.

A woman's voice: *"Echo 3, Echo 3. Diaz. Stanley. What's your 20, over."*

I'm fumbling at the thing . . .

"Diaz, what's your—"

I kill the call.

"What was this?"

I shake my head. "Nothing. I picked up a radio. Signals get crossed all the time."

Sense her staring at me in profile. I don't turn. "Okay. Scared me," she says.

Check the rearview. Hakim Stanley rides quietly in the back, his single eye. No. I look through him. The Nissan and the Lincoln are hanging back but certainly with us. Convoy style upriver.

Iveta is peering out the window. "I have never been to Bronx."

278 to the Bronx River Parkway, the Nissan and the Navigator still a good ways back. Exit 9 to Gun Hill Road.

Here comes the prodigal son.

Put the key in the door. It turns easily. The air in here is stale, but the place is spotless. Window shades drawn tight. It's a two-bedroom job. I feel nothing for it.

I do a quick check of the apartment, gun drawn but held low. Single mattress on the floor of the larger bedroom. Check the bathroom, suitcase in hand. Close the door.

Drop an object in a ziplock bag. Stand on the toilet, gently remove the screen to the vent. Carefully set the object down within. Replace the metal screen. Hop down. Exit bathroom.

"Is this safe neighborhood?" calls Iveta.

Back in the main area. I shrug and make a so-so gesture. "Depends on your definition of safe."

Iveta drops her bag. "What is this place?" Opens the refrigerator, which is empty, clean-ish, and not plugged in.

"Used to live here."

"When?"

"Awhile back."

"Live alone?"

"No."

Iveta stares at me for a bit. Nods, leaves it at that.

I consider my plan. I consider the wisdom of leaving her alone here. That aspect of the whole thing is deeply flawed. But I decide it's the best I can do.

May God protect her.

Iveta reading my mind. "So, Mr. Decimal. What happens now?" she says. Like that.

Me, I'm standing there with the briefcase, pig-sweating in the Kevlar vest.

It's not her mouth, her expression. Something about her posture. Says we could call a time out. Maybe, just perhaps, discover comfort, quiet, a spot to rest, if only for a finite period. Within each other.

But no. To my eternal dismay, I hear myself: "Now what happens is I go straighten this out. You stay put. Sleep if you have to, but double-lock the door and keep your gun in sight. Don't open the blinds."

Iveta is saying something but I miss it as I close the door behind me.

Out of the building and past the playground, eating a pill as I go. I'm holding my breath, holding the briefcase under my arm, and pulling on the surgical gloves.

Don't see the tail convoy, but I bet they're around. Gotta pull them away from Iveta. Into the Prius. Deep breath.

I gun it out of the parking lot. Thinking: follow me. Follow me, please.

Hakim Stanley rides in the back, silent. As fast as I drive, I doubt if I'll ditch him.

Heading east on Gun Hill, gliding on through the flashing yellow lights. Think maybe I was tripping. About that Nissan. Maybe I was reading too much into things, frazzled as I am. And there's plenty of Navis. I'm shook up. Iveta, she throws me. Hate to be seen like this, thrashing around, flailing like a newborn.

I'm thinking such stuff, but that's until I near Van Cortlandt Park. Then I clock familiar headlights. Back a ways but it's definitely the blue Nissan. Followed up shortly by lights that, judging by their height and spacing, are likely to be the Navigator.

Okay then.

I hit 87 going southeast. The Nissan and Navigator still with me. I accelerate. Granted, it's a Prius. But I floor the fucker.

The Nissan does likewise. The Navi falls back.

We streak by the crust of the old Yankee Stadium to the left, I think about that Down syndrome kid. Push it away. Stanley rides with me though, nothing I can do. Try to catch his eye in the rearview, he won't look at me. He mouths, *You.*

The Prius is just barely in control. I'm all over the road. These cars, man, they must be fucking joking with these cars.

So shit. Let's see how my friend or friends dig on Harlem. I make like I'm headed straight, but at the last possible moment I aim at the exit ramp on the right, missing a concrete divider by inches. Down the hill and up again, a hard right onto the 138th Street Bridge. I can smell rubber, even on top of the Stench.

The Nissan is up my ass the whole way. Effortless. It's for sure got more torque, more power. I try to get a look at the driver but I have to concentrate on not sailing off the road. Bear left now, I'm leaning into it like I'm on a bike. Coming down the off-ramp that will terminate in 135th Street, I see the opportunity I had hoped for.

I prepare to brake, the Prius listing left and right. As we hit the bottom of the ramp, I stamp on the brakes, go into a semicontrolled spin, pinwheeling to the right. Hear the Nissan braking as well, I slide to a stop at an angle, blocking both lanes of traffic.

The Nissan has come to rest about ten feet up the hill, directly facing me. I try not to dilly-dally, I get my ass down, I'm out of the car with the Sig, go low around the door, lean across the hood, get a good look despite the headlights directly in my face, and shoot out the front two tires on the Nissan, *pop, pop*.

Duck back behind the car. Give it a second, then

peek over the hood. Headlights at the top of the hill, and the Navigator bounces around the corner.

The doors on the Nissan come open on both sides, I estimate two guys exit the car, hard to see much beyond the glare of its headlights.

The Lincoln comes to stop at a discreet distance. I duck back down. Love to get a do-over on this.

"FBI!" calls one of the dudes, crouching behind the Nissan's door. "Drop the weapon and lay down on the ground, let's not have this get any worse than it already is!"

Some action-movie shit. Drop my weapon? Not likely. I don't bother responding.

I hear a gang of shoes slapping down the off-ramp. I peek again, there's a flock of suits, four additional men, armed like Mexican drug runners. Apparently they're not shy cause bullets commence pinging off my hood, not sure who's firing but I try to lower myself, and crab it to the left, so I'm in front of the tire.

Positive hailstorm of bullets. Jesus. I don't have a next move. Somebody's yelling something and the volley tapers and stops.

I look under the car. The tires facing out on the Prius are all "shhh," perforated, history.

Bullhorn crackle. "*Gonna ask you again to put down your weapon and lay on the ground. You have thirty seconds to comply or we move in on you.*"

Christ, I really have no options. Reckon: I should just rock it and go out in a blaze of glory, a big fat gun in each hand. But the impulse to live trumps everything. I'm afraid this is true.

"All right," I find myself saying. "Okay. Look, I'm going to place my weapons on the hood of the car and then stand up with my hands on my head, okay? No shooting me, okay? I'm cooperating."

There's a pause, I guess they're conferring.

Bullhorn feedback and click. "*Okay, let's do it just like that. If you come up with anything resembling a weapon, we'll be forced to open fire. Do everything slow. Go ahead.*"

Is this really how I want to do this thing? No. But sometimes you have to know your limits. And I hope I'm right about that.

So, I set the Sig Sauer on the Toyota's hood, followed by the Beretta. Placing my hands on top of my head, I gradually stand. My bad leg is asleep.

Guys running, coming around the side of the Prius, I'm thrown on the hood. My hat rolls off. Damnit. If my cheekbone wasn't broken before, it is now.

Handcuffs close over my wrists, not for the first time this week. They're pulling my stuff out of my pants and jacket and tossing it on the hood . . . my ID, my Homeland badge, the locker keycard, my pills. All my gear.

"Is this the piece of dogshit who got Anne?" says one guy.

"Yeah, it's him. Lemme," responds another. Mike, was it? Japanese dude. Or whatever.

Sure it's Mike, because he says, "Hey, bitch."

"Who the fuck are you talking to?" I say.

"Step aside for a second."

"Hey, gentlemen—"

A crisp punch to my kidneys shuts me up. Back facing the hood of the car now. Another punch lands. Then another. Another. I'm getting pummeled here.

I turn my face to the right and puke. Again. A string

of bile. I don't count the number of hits he gets in, but the guy honestly lets me have it. I start to drift.

"All right, hold it! Agent Shimosato!"

The beating stops. I'm pulled up by my hair.

"That," says Agent Mike in my ear, "was for Anne, you bastard fuck."

"Oh man, did you have a thing with Anne?" I manage to say. "Make no mistake, sugar, she kicked *my* ass into next week, not the other way around."

"Agent Shimosato!"

In my ear: "We're not done. Believe that."

Then I'm manhandled around the car. Up the incline to the Navigator.

"Grab his stuff," somebody says.

I just see blue suits and guns, the door to the Navigator is opened and I'm tossed in the backseat.

"So. Hello," says the man opposite me.

I look up, bleary, and am met by thick glasses and a tracksuit. Brian, Brian Petrovic. Unsurprisingly.

My shit is dumped on the floor of the Navigator, briefcase, guns, and all. The door is slammed shut.

It's quiet for a bit. Then, "Won't make the same mistake twice," says Brian. Smiles. Picks up my guns.

I'm on my side, but through the smoke-tinted glass I idly register two federales high-fiving each other. Whooping. Touchdown, like.

Brian doesn't register this. Clears his throat. "So, so," says the man, "Let's have a look." He picks up the briefcase. "Combination."

I don't say anything. I'm in a lot of pain.

He smiles and looks at me sideways. "Come now. Combination?"

I drag myself up into a sitting position, gritting my teeth. "Six-six-six," I tell him, cause what am I going to be, clever now?

He chuckles at that. Twiddles the lock, opens the case. "So. Did you perhaps get my note?"

"I did."

"And your thoughts on this . . ."

"I'm not feeling like the deal is particularly favorable to me."

The man is quiet for a bit, nods. "When we last met, there was I think some confusion." He peeps the night-vision goggles, frowns, sets them aside.

"Oh yeah? What was that?"

Brian takes a box of bullets out of the case, places them next to him. He folds his hands and leans forward. "So. Multiple things, really. The first being you stole my property. This has caused me a lot of problems. You can never comprehend how important this object is to my people. And to me personally, as a broker."

"I'm listening."

"So. So, you see, I had an individual, a buyer for that particular piece and he was very unhappy to hear that it has disappeared. I have to delay my trip abroad till this is settled."

"I'm sorry to hear that."

Brian looks at me. "You have endangered me. This man, this buyer. He is very unhappy. I want to keep myself from bigger problems, so I want my property back."

"I can understand. It sounds stressful."

Brian has Yakiv's file open. He's squinting at it, turns on the overhead lights in the back. He flips through the file, frowning, flips back to the front. Slowly, a grin works its way across his face. He holds up the file, taps it. "So. Another issue I am dealing with, as matter of fact, concerns this man."

Huh. I wait for it.

"I'm told you have abducted him. No? Something crazy. So, so, you walk into his place, just take him, shoot your way out. Cowboy. This is true?"

I shrug.

"Well, so, if it's true, you might know where he is located."

My brain is working hard. I don't respond.

"Mr. Decimal? Do you know who this man is? What he's done?"

"I have some idea."

Brian clears his throat. "Just for perspective . . . he entered U.S. in 2000 with his wife and two children. He is wanted by many, many different entities in several countries for his crimes."

I nod. "Yes, that's all in the files there, I'm aware of that."

Brian smiles. "But. So. I am thinking, you're still confused."

"How you reckon that?"

"This day we met, at this church."

"Yes?"

"The name you called me."

"I was addressing you by what I understand to be your given name."

Brian shakes his head. "This man," he says, indicating the file, "*this* man is our Branko Jokanovic."

Hang on a minute. I'm trying to pull this all together.

"So who the fuck does that make you?" I ask, and it's deeply lame. I'm out of sorts here.

Brian coughs. Or laughs, can't tell which. "So, so, I'm just a procurer. Brian Petrovic. Middleman. Working with various government agencies. Working with your FBI on international matters. So, but, I have, on the side, this . . . extra work. Mostly deals with art and things such as this. So, this is where I am making my living, and the people I deal with here, they are not so . . . forgiving. I am fortunate to have these agents here, willing to make some extra time to join with me on these projects. Extra time for extra pay, of course."

"Sounds, uh, like a sweet setup . . . but I still . . . What about this Yakiv?"

"We put word out via government channels and the general criminal circle that I was Branko, this was good because it makes real Branko relax, and perhaps makes him, a, what do you say, a softer target." He smiles at me, a sad smile. "But official work with Interpol and FBI, this is sort of like public service. To find men and women like Branko Jokanovic. Like the woman you've just secured at this apartment in the Bronx."

I'm listening. I'm listening hard.

See, I don't give a fuck about Yakiv/Branko, whoever. I did what I did under the correct assumption that he was a mass-murdering war criminal. The name thing doesn't make a difference.

But Iveta. My fingers start to tingle as I overbreathe.

"Which," says the man, "brings us to the other major concern, so. As per my note."

"She has nothing to do with—"

"Mr. Decimal, I'm very sorry, but she has everything

to do with this. She is Branko's wife. She, like Branko, is wanted in several countries for grievous crimes. Did you not know this?"

I look at my hands, still gloved. I am watching this scene play out as if from far above my body.

"So, so. She has you thinking something else, hmm?" He offers another melancholy smile. "What has she told you, my confused friend?"

"There has been some sort of mistake here . . ."

"Well. So. You are very confused indeed. This doesn't bother me, if you are confused. But for yourself, what you should be concerned with is to tell me a) where are the 'Shapskos,' Mr. and Mrs. and b) where is the box. Otherwise, we have bigger problems than you can imagine."

I'm nodding. My lips have gone numb. I look at the yellow keycard on the SUV's floor. "How would you feel," I say slowly, "about working out some sort of alternate exchange?"

Six pairs of dress shoes clap across the marble of Grand Central Station, ping-ponging off the walls like a beginner's tap class.

"Here." We have arrived at the bank of lockers. "It's number 14, the second set." Get it? Two. Fourteen. Easy to remember. I'd point it out for them but I've still got the cuffs on.

Brian takes the card and looks at it dubiously. Hands it to Agent Mike, who gives me a shitty look, walks over, and inserts it in the slot for the correct locker. He then opens it, and steps aside.

Suddenly the FBI folks are looking anywhere but Brian, all nonchalant.

Brian steps forward, withdraws a plastic bag, looks at me. "So. This had better be what I think it is."

I nod. "Have a look."

The older man withdraws the wooden box. Examines it, feels the markings like braille. Smells it. Slides open the side and has a good long gander at the hand within. After a time, he nods to himself and smiles.

I realize I haven't been breathing.

Brian approaches me, putting the box back in the bag. "You must understand. This is not about religion. For us, it is a thing of national pride. We have so little. So, so, God gives us these priceless gifts." He's lost in a fog for a second, then snaps back. "Despite the difficulties you present earlier, you've just saved me much . . .

inconvenience. And pain. So. And made everyone here some money."

I nod.

"The buyer is in Paris, I likely go tomorrow then, so, so. But. What about the other matter?"

"Give me a pen and a bit of paper. And uncuff me, if you would."

Brian looks at his guys. "So, who has a pen? And keys for these things?"

One of the fellows is behind me removing the cuffs, another hands me a pen and a tiny notebook.

I rub my wrists, then write the following:

Chelsea Market, 9th Ave btw W. 15th + W. 16th
Chelsea Wine Vault
Basemen thru trapdoor behind register

Brian looks at this. Raises his eyebrows.

I say, "You didn't specify as to dead or alive."

Brian shakes his head. "No, I didn't. Alive is always better, people get some peace, so, so, *closure*, like you Americans say so much. But either way. I get paid the same."

I nod at the notebook. "Go to that location. If things aren't as I describe, the deal is off and you can do what you need to do. But I think you'll find some, what, some closure there."

Brian is quiet, staring at the notebook. Then he moves closer to me. "Speaking of closure. My information. Much of it I got from a man you know. Here, in New York. A man who is your . . . sometimes employer, hmm?"

"Are we talking about the district attorney?"

He makes an unreadable head gesture. "These titles. Who can say? All I am telling to you is he is making things easier for me, this local government man. Seems to have some . . . personal motivation, I think. Interested in seeing these two disappear. I don't know reasons why. Just for you to know. So, so. Do what you want with that."

"Was he your point person here in the city?"

"Not until recently, but these last days, so, he feeds me information. Yes."

"I guess what I'm getting at: how extensive is the list of people who can ID Branko and his wife?"

Brian shrugs. "I would think very, very limited. Definitely this man I speak of now. Also some CIA people overseas. And of course, this lovely couple's victims. So. But they can hardly speak up now, can they?" He gives me an ugly grin.

I'm thinking: uh-huh.

"Anyway," says Brian, "you won't see me again, if this all is, hmm, checking out here." He taps the address I gave him. "So, I am done in this city."

I extend my hand. "Do we have a deal?"

There's a pause. "Yes," says Brian simply.

We shake. I'm given my gear. The agents part. And I am on my way, strapping on my guns as I go.

This time, up at the Trump Tower, I go through the service entrance, unobserved. Been neglecting the System. With the System, pathways become clear. Easiest thing in the world.

Walk though a dark kitchen to a stairwell. Climb it to the eleventh floor. Swap out my surgical gloves for a new pair.

I knock three times at number 1119. Wait. Knock louder.

Daniel opens the door, disheveled, in a brown bathrobe. "Decimal. Goddamnit. I can't sleep." Gin comes off him in syrupy waves.

I walk in, past him. He weeble-wobbles a bit.

"I, uh, have been waiting. Thinking. About us, all this nonsense."

I'm looking at him in the dark. He turns a light on. Has to reach for it a couple times before he manages.

"Decimal. Look. Bygones and all that. Fuck it. We got a thing together. That's bigger than. I just . . . You wanna drink?"

I follow him into a decent-size office/living area. Computer, papers, lots of files. A dumpy couch, fireplace. He's got a miniature fridge and a fully stocked wet bar.

"What can I get you? Dewey. Let's have a drink, fuck it."

I take out the Sig Sauer. I just take it out, don't point it anywhere.

"I'm unarmed," he says.

I produce the silencer.

"Dewey. Wow. It's amazing. What we can convince ourselves of. She's got you thinking, what? That in getting me out of the way, what, gonna solve all your problems. Am I right? When I'm right, I'm right."

"Daniel. You need to shut your fucking mouth. You're making this worse." I'm attaching the silencer.

"Decimal. Look at me." He sways a bit. "Will you give me two minutes? Straighten this out? It's actually very simple." His hand is trembling. "Decimal."

"I'm listening. Won't make any difference."

"The stuff I said. About physically, uh, harming you. You know, I gave this reconsideration. Want you to know. Nothing to be worried about there."

No response from me.

He's sweating it, tries another approach. "Listen. This fucking broad. You've been misled. That's fine. Me too. Look. Need you to know." He waves his hand at the stack of papers near his desk. "Top of that pile. There's a file, behind you. Everything you need to know about the woman we have called Iveta. It's really bad-news kind of shit. She's . . . Decimal, I'm telling you the truth. Right now. She has us both fooled. Playing us against each other. From the jump. Decimal."

I pull his desk chair around from behind his desk. "Have a seat," I say. He plops down in the chair. I'm standing over him.

"You gotta know. I met her at one of these goddamn parties. Very persuasive. Plus I'm flattered, you know? Don't draw ladies like I used to. Anyway. I was, you know, hook, line, and sinker. The whole nine. I mean hell. They were living separate lives. Like me and my ex. Figured, get the husband out of the picture. Safety's sake. Bring my best man in. That's you. The best. Then, fuck's sake, somebody at the State Department drops a dime on the pair of them. Sends this paperwork through. You can imagine. That it turns into this. My shock. So I gotta, I gotta make it right. Decimal. Say something."

I pull back the hammer and raise the gun to his forehead. A stain spreads across his lap, he's pissed himself, drink or fear or both, but to his credit, maintains eye contact and keeps his voice steady.

"Decimal. Under her file. You'll find *your own* file. I think you might want to have a long look at that too. I admit," he says, taking a deep breath. "I admit I took advantage. So fucking sue me. Your situation. You're confused. The pills. They're sugar, they're nothing. You've had a lot of bad breaks. But you're not what you think you are. Decimal. You're a lot. Of fucking things. But you're not this, this person in your head."

"Are you through, Rosenblatt?"

"No. Decimal. There was never a wife and child. Decimal. Just went with the story. The story you had going. Followed your narrative. You have a whole mythology. I just went with it. But it's all been, what. Imposed on you."

I won't hear this. I don't hear this.

"So I'm thinking, you and me. Bring the biggest motherfucker of a lawsuit. The military has ever laid eyes on. Decimal, your file. You gotta know. The stuff they did. They opened up your fuckin *brain* . . ."

No, I won't hear this. "That's enough. It's not working," I say.

"You're not—"

"Rosenblatt, you're about to die. Do you understand?"

"You're not. A freaking monster."

I shoot him then, his balding scalp, and he goes floppy. Blood and other viscous stuff hit the far wall. His bowels evacuate, I smell it. Cuts through the plastic.

Dan, I am the sick black monster under your bed. I'm a stone-cold badass freak motherfucker of a baby killer. Doing what I groove on, what I do best.

That's who I am and that's how I do it.

Set my gun down behind me, on top of the file folders. Get out the digi camera, lens cap off. Too much backlight. I wanna capture the moment.

I get a shot of him, side on. As always, it's an anticlimax. If it weren't for all the blood, you'd think he was sleeping.

I pick up my gun, revealing the words:

International War Crimes Tribunal, The Hague, Netherlands—Classified Material

I'm thinking, just leave it be. Better to not know. But of course I flip open the folder.

Right there on page one, a candid shot of Iveta. No makeup, considerably younger. Military uniform and cap. Her hand is raised, she is indicating something to two uniformed men. The name underneath the photo reads, *Jovana Rac, Pristina, Kosovo, 1998.*

I'd like to believe this is cheap shit, an amateur forgery. I know it's not. Flip the page.

The heading is *Prepared for INTERPOL by the ICTY.*

Read:

. . . Jovana Rac is remarkable in the sense that women were an extreme rarity in the Serbian military forces, otherwise

noted for their misogyny. Her usefulness is perhaps illustrated by the charges raised against her.

Rac is accused of furnishing women and girls for convicted war criminal Radomir Kovac and for contractors at CYNACORP for the purposes of sexual enslavement and forced labor; and of involvement with so-called "rape camps" in the region of Foca. Additionally, Rac is accused of one count of genocide, and of human trafficking.

I'm starting to feel sick. I close the file, look at the cover, look at the photo again . . . go back to the second page.

. . . active and enthusiastic participant in Operation Horseshoe, a large-scale campaign of ethnic cleansing of Kosovo Albanians. Rac was detained by NATO forces on August 17, 1999.

More photos, mug shots: face-on and face left/right. The hair is shorter still, but it's her. The caption is: *Jovana Rac, August 18, 1999.*

God, she looks great though.

I flip a few pages more, my fingers tingling. I lose my peripheral vision and am overbreathing. Disembodied, I see myself, reading this, landing on:

Escaped September 3, 1999, as a military transport to International War Crimes Tribunal for the former Yugoslavia, The Hague, Netherlands, was diverted to Kishinev, Moldova, due to poor weather conditions. She has been traced as far as Odessa, Ukraine. Current whereabouts are unknown.

I stop turning the pages. My head knows this is no forgery. I understand I needed to see this. My heart asks the obvious question: is this the woman for whom you have marinated me in blood? Is this the creature you would seek to protect?

Hakim Stanley watches me from the corner. Smiling. I know what he's thinking.

I close the file, pick it up.

I close my eyes. Stand there for a while, like that.

Place my gun in my mouth. It's still hot, tastes like chemicals. I pull back the hammer.

But that doesn't feel right. No, nothing is that simple. It'd be cheating.

I withdraw my pistol and open my eyes.

In picking up Jovana's file, I have exposed another. It's cover reads:

Walter Reed—National Institutes of Health

That would be me.

Hell no. I take both dossiers. I extract one sheet, the photocopied mug shot of Jovana. I pocket this.

At the wet bar I grab a bottle of vodka. Drop both files in the fireplace. Douse them in vodka.

Matches on the heath, strike them, *poof*. Flames consume paper.

Pull off the gloves. Get out the Purell™, scrub up.

Based on this new information, I might need to rethink my current plans.

I pop a pill, and Hakim and I wait and watch the fire until it's all gone.

The playground. The garbage. It's all there. It's always been there. Outside of the projects, properly named the Gun Hill Houses.

It's me outside the projects, just as I was on my return from figurative padded rooms in D.C.

Biopsies, drip IVs. Catheter tubes. Nonsense questionnaires. A rainbow of pastel capsules and pills. Isolation tanks. Electrical charges. High-pressure hoses. Induced headaches. Neon green tracer fluids coursing through the body. Restraints. Merciless fluorescent lighting.

Note that none of this matters now. Disregard it. The System maps out my future movements.

Enter the building. All surfaces are subway-car metallic, reflecting the warped form that is me. Enter the elevator and a cloud of piss and beer. Push the correct button.

All of this is deeply familiar. Exit the elevator, follow the hallway to the correct door. Take out the key. Enter the bedroom. Pistol is drawn.

Stanley hovers in a darkened corner, a shadow. Blinks his single eye.

Iveta/Jovana sleeps beneath a worn sheet.

Watch the sheet rise and fall. Rise and fall.

Two options, both simple and easily done. Either way it ends badly for me.

I choose option B. Lift the gun. Engage the safety.

I take the page from Jovana's file out of my pocket, unfold it, and set it beside the mattress. Place the key to the apartment on top of it. On the back I have written: *Jovana. FBI/INTERPOL knows. I know. Time to go.*

Take a last look at her. She appears so small. I can only see the top of her head.

On my way out, I withdraw the plastic bag from the bathroom vent. Avoiding the mirror, knowing who I'll see there.

Close the door behind me, quiet as possible.

Twenty-sixth Street near Sixth Avenue.

The prehistoric parishioners start straggling in, so I reckon services at the Cathedral of Saint Sava are soon to be getting underway.

I spritz a little Purell™ on my hands. Rub it in.

This idea here came to me late last night.

Taking a welcome break from the 000 of computer science/general works, I had been doing some reading on the Serbian Orthodox Church, so it was fresh on the brain.

Woke up this morning and thought, hell, it seems like a nice day for a walk regardless.

I got here via a series of left turns. You know me. You know how I do.

Adjust my hat. Feeling way out of place.

"Sir, you had asked to see me?"

I point myself in the speaker's direction. It's the same dude from my previous visit, and like all the best priests he's clad in black from head to toe, even in this goddamn heat.

"Yes, I did. Don't know what the protocol is here, so I'll just get to it."

I produce the ziplock, the mummified hand within.

"This, well, I believe belongs to your institution. Not this particular church, but the denomination in general. Sorry about the . . . the packaging."

He looks at the thing in confusion. "Is this a joke, sir?"

"No, it is not. This is, you know," I jiggle the bag, "'the hand.' Or whatever." I mime the quotes in the air.

He gets it now. His substantial monobrow nearly hits his hairline. "For the love of . . . And I suppose you believe you can sell me this thing?"

I shake my head. People assuming shit, I swear. "Just here to return it. That's all. What am I gonna do with it? I don't know what you people get up to with these deals, but I can appreciate that they're important to you."

He looks from me to the baggie and back to me.

"So, here." I hand him the ziplock.

He takes it. "There were stories," he says quietly. "I heard it went missing, during these endless wars, of course . . ."

"Well, it was presented to me as the real deal. Carbon dating, X-rays. I don't know how you actually confirm shit like that. Pardon me, Padre." Shouldn't be cursing in church.

He sticks out his hand. We shake. I see his eyes are welling up, which seems to be embarrassing for both of us.

"Please . . ." he says. "Won't you stay for the service?" He indicates a nearby pew.

I think about that. It is the weekend, after all. My books can wait, they've waited this long. And it's hot as fuck out, that nasty wet New York heat.

"Yeah," I say. "Yeah, sure, why not."

"What is your name, my friend, so I can dedicate a specific prayer. So that God may protect and continue to bestow His blessings."

I want to say, *Iveta*. I want to say, *Hakim Stanley*. But I say, "Decimal. Dewey Decimal."

"Dewey Decimal," he repeats. "Thank you." He dabs at his eyes and splits.

Probably has a warm-up kind of thing he does, get himself psyched up to represent for God.

I watch the old biddies inch forward to take their positions. Enjoy that incense.

Thinking, motherfucker, I'm so glad I didn't off myself. I have a lot of living to do up in this bitch.

Wonder where Jovana is right now, right at this very moment.

Wonder about Stanley. His family.

A minute later I sit, pop a pill.

Damn, these pews are comfortable. Despite the multitude of microscopic parasites and bacteria that reside in the wood, residue of asses past.

A hush comes over the place as the service begins, like gauze dropped over my head.

And I sleep.

Also available from Akashic Books

THE DEAD DETECTIVE
a novel by William Heffernan
320 pages, hardcover original, $24.95

"*The Dead Detective* is William Heffernan's first novel in seven years, and wherever he's been, he hasn't forgotten how to write a good, gritty police procedural . . . This edgy police drama succeeds in capturing the hysteria that grips Tampa residents when a celebrity criminal . . . is found dead in a cypress swamp with her throat cut and the word 'Evil' carved into her forehead."
—*New York Times Book Review*

"*The Dead Detective* is a meaty story that offers an intriguing and conflicted protagonist, a darkly fascinating victim, solid police procedural detail, a knowing look at the Tampa Bay area and its politics, an unlikely murderer, and a creepy denouement that hints that Harry [protagonist] will be back." —*Booklist*

BLACK ORCHID BLUES
a novel by Persia Walker
272 pages, trade paperback original, $15.95

"The best kind of historical mystery: great history, great mystery, all wrapped up in a voice so authentic you feel it has come out of the past to whisper in your ear."
—Lee Child, author of *Worth Dying For*

"A remarkable achievement; imagine the richly provocative atmosphere of Walter Mosley or James Ellroy's best period work, and a savvy, truly likable heroine, and you have *Black Orchid Blues.* Persia Walker is a rising superstar in the mystery genre."
—Jason Starr, best-selling author of *The Pack*

THE PRICE OF ESCAPE
a novel by David Unger
224 pages, trade paperback original, $15.95

"David Unger spins a fascinating tale of weird redemption in *The Price of Escape,* leading us on a tense journey from 1938 Nazi Germany all the way to Guatemala. The sinister United Fruit Company casts a giant shadow over this vividly rendered landscape, devouring everyone and everything in its path. Unger has created a compelling protagonist in the flawed and anguished Samuel Berkow, a man on the run from his own demons and the terrible forces of history."
—Jessica Hagedorn, author of *Dream Jungle*